Keep Her S

Also by Kiki Swinson

The Score
Playing Dirty
Notorious
Wifey
I'm Still Wifey
Life After Wifey
Still Wifey Material
A Sticky Situation
The Candy Shop
Wife Extraordinaire
Wife Extraordinaire Returns
Cheaper to Keep Her
Cheaper to Keep Her 2

Anthologies
Sleeping with the Enemy (with Wahida Clark)
Heist (with De'nesha Diamond)
Heist 2 (with De'nesha Diamond)
Lifestyles of the Rich and Shameless (with Noire)
A Gangster and a Gentleman
(with De'nesha Diamond)
Most Wanted (with Nikki Turner)
Still Candy Shopping (with Amaleka McCall)
Fistful of Benjamins (with De'nesha Diamond)

Published by Kensington Publishing Corp.

Cheaper to Keep Her 3

KIKI SWINSON

Kensington Publishing Corp.
http://www.kensingtonbooks.com

DAFINA BOOKS are published by

Kensington Publishing Corp.
119 West 40th Street
New York, NY 10018

Copyright © 2012 by Kiki Swinson

All Kensington Titles, Imprints, and Distributed Lines are available at special quantity discounts for bulk purchases for sales promotions, premiums, fund-raising, and educational or institutional use. Special book excerpts or customized printings can also be created to fit specific needs. For details, write or phone the office of the Kensington special sales manager: Kensington Publishing Corp., 119 West 40th Street, New York, NY 10018, attn: Special Sales Department, Phone: 1-800-221-2647.

Dafina and the Dafina logo Reg. U.S. Pat. & TM Off.

ISBN-13: 978-1-4967-0072-8
ISBN-10: 1-4967-0072-4
First Kensington Mass Market Edition: March 2016

10 9 8 7 6 5 4 3 2 1

Printed in the United States of America

Chapter 1

My New Stomping Grounds

Leaving Virginia to go with Bishop to New Jersey was the best decision I could've made. While Bishop, Torch, Monty, and I were in transit, I went through my cell phone, transferred a few important phone numbers on paper, including Lil Rodney's cell phone number, and then I discarded it from our moving vehicle. Rodney was a young cat from my old neighborhood, but he had enough clout to get shit down when he needed to. He covered my ass when I sat back on the sidelines to watch Diamond and the second time when I brought Bishop and his team back to handle their business. So I planned to reach out to him later to get the 411 on what was going on back in Virginia, since I knew he kept his ears to the streets. Nothing got past Lil Rodney, and everyone knew it.

Other than that, Bishop has shown me around his hometown of Newark for the past two months, and I admit that I have loved every minute of it. He introduced me to a couple of cats he hung out with from time to time, and I even met his sister, Bria, after he posted the money she needed to get out of jail. I heard through various conversations Bishop had with the cats in his circle that Bria was pulled over in a traffic stop by local police and was busted and charged with possession of a couple grams of heroin and ten thousand dollars in cash. Bishop was more upset about the money than he was about the dope. Either way you looked at it, he lost out twice.

My first visit to Bria's house was somewhat pleasant. She seemed cool, but she came across to me like she was a stripper. In my years of being around strippers, I had known them to be cunning and scandalous. They acted like they had game on the surface, but underneath all that makeup and cheap-ass lingerie, those hoes were dumb as a thirty-year-old nigga in the fifth grade.

During our formal introduction, she smiled and I instantly saw a strong resemblance to

Neeko. I swear it scared the hell out of me. She and I spoke briefly about where I was from and how long I would be in town. I found her to be too inquisitive for words. She wanted to know everything, from how Bishop and I met, what day we met, and whether I had intentions to get serious with him. I started to tell her to mind her damn business, but I decided against it when Bishop interrupted our chat and told her to stop being nosy. She ended up leaving me alone and chimed in on him. "When are you going to put me back on the payroll? You know I need the money so I can pay my lawyer," she told him.

I'm not the one for making assumptions, but I knew what she meant when she asked him to put her back on the payroll. But Bishop wasn't feeling that conversation at all and immediately left the room. She seemed humiliated after he left her standing there. I wanted to say something, but I just didn't know what to say.

After one hour into the visit, Bria started acting really weird, and Bishop finally told me that it was time to go. So, I said my good-byes to Bria and then we got out of there. But I have to say that my overall visit with Bria was somewhat cool. She acted like she was on drugs, which was probably why Bishop stopped her from making moves on behalf of him. Things were definitely coming to the light for him.

There were some things he liked and some things he didn't like, so he dealt with them accordingly. And when it was all said and done, I was rolling with Bishop because he was the one that paid the bills.

For the first three weeks in Jersey, Bishop had me staying at an Extended Stay hotel. And then he found me a one-bedroom spot about twenty miles from where he resided with his main chick, Keisha. Bishop didn't grant me the privilege of meeting Keisha, but that bitch made it her business to call Bishop every time he was in my company. Like today, for instance, he and I were eating lunch at this little spot inside of Jersey Gardens Outlet Mall when she called and got really irate. I couldn't hear everything she was saying, but I heard her screaming through the phone. Thirty seconds into her rant, Bishop said, "Keisha, I don't have time for this shit right now!"

Keisha yelled back through the phone, and before she finished saying whatever she had to say, Bishop disconnected their call. I sat there in my chair and wondered what she said that made him upset. I wanted so badly to ask him, but I decided against it. I'd known Bishop only a few months, and in that short time I found out that he was an extremely private person. Very seldom could you get him to answer a few questions, so I left well enough alone.

I continued eating away at my slice of cheese-cake, and when I was done he asked me if I was ready to continue shopping. When I assured him that I was, we got up and headed toward the Burberry store. It was early spring, which means a lot of rain, so I asked Bishop to purchase a five hundred dollar raincoat for me. Money was no object to him, so he practically gave me everything I asked for.

Before we walked over to the checkout counter, Bishop pulled his wallet from his pocket and opened it. I couldn't believe my eyes when I saw a Virginia driver's license that belonged to my ex–best friend, Diamond. Her face was magnified on the ID card the longer I stared at it. I couldn't help but wonder why Bishop had it, so I asked him, and his response was, "When I get rid of people who are a threat to me, I always take their ID cards."

"Why?" I continued. I needed to know why he'd take such a huge risk to hold on to his victims' driver's licenses.

He smiled as if he found humor in our conversation. "Look, don't take this the wrong way, but I feel that it's necessary that I take all the ID cards from the people I snuff, because that'll make the police work extra hard to identify their bodies. And then on top of that, I get to keep their IDs as souvenirs."

I gave Bishop a blank facial expression. I

couldn't believe the words that had come out of his mouth. He sounded just like a fucking psycho. Was he for real? I hoped he was joking. "Well, don't you think that that's a little too risky? What if the cops pulled you over in a traffic stop, how would you explain to them why you have her ID, or anyone else's ID for that matter?"

"Look, Lynise, I can't worry about that now. I'm a firm believer that when shit happens, it happens for a reason and we can't do anything about it. So stop being all paranoid. Everything is going to be all right," he assured me, and then he moved Diamond's driver's license to the back of his wallet.

After he gave me the money to pay for the raincoat, he told me he'd meet me outside of the store. I watched him as he walked away from me and wondered whether I was really ready to be with this guy. He was definitely a sweetheart and a protector, but I got this gut feeling that I might be in over my head. Okay, sure, he bought me some clothes, he had put me up in a hotel, he fed me, and he even saved my life back in Virginia. But it wasn't just a one-way street. I looked out for his ass too. And I provided a sense of loyalty to him. I figured as long as he had my back and never disrespected me, we'd forever be on easy street. But the minute he tries to play me, all bets are off. I'll go into bitch mode and he won't like that side of me. Not too many niggas I fucked with in the past hadn't saw that side of me, because I was gullible as hell. But I'd grown a tough skin in these recent months, so he'd better watch out.

Right after I paid for my merchandise, I exited the store and met up with Bishop in the middle of the mall, and then we headed over to the Lacoste store. Bishop said he wanted to get a few shirts from there, so I helped him pick them out.

On our way out of the store, a full-figured woman approached us with two other women in tow and started screaming at Bishop. Immediately after she opened her mouth I knew it was Keisha. But I was taken aback a little by her appearance. I'd never thought Bishop was attracted to big girls. He seemed like the type who'd only date chicks like me or maybe just a few pounds bigger. Well, I guess I didn't know him after all.

While I stood there quiet as a mouse, I took inventory of Keisha's overall appearance. She was a pretty, brown-skinned woman. She was about five feet seven, and I loved the way she wore her hair. She rocked the silk wrap. But her wardrobe definitely needed a facelift. Her two friends were my height and size, but they weren't attractive at all. I figured one woman couldn't have it all, and in that case I was truly blessed.

"I knew it!" she spat as she got within two feet of us. "I knew you were fucking around on me with some low-budget bitch!"

The fact that she'd just called me a bitch warranted that she get the shit smacked out of her, but since she had her little entourage with her and there was only one of me, I kept my cool and allowed Bishop to handle her big, goofy-looking ass.

"Keisha, you better get your ass out of my face right now and take your ass back home. You know I don't play this type of game," he said calmly. He was desperately trying to keep a lid on the confrontation with his woman.

"And you know I don't play these fucking games either. Got this bitch parading around the fucking mall with bags from Burberry and Saks. Whatcha took her shopping for, so you can fuck her stinky ass later?" she barked.

I swear I couldn't take it any longer. This had gotten personal. She had just called me a bitch for the second time and I had to do something about it. "First of all, I ain't gon' be too many more bitches! And whether or not he's going to fuck me after we leave here is none of your business being as though I don't see a ring on your finger!" I snapped as I pointed my finger in her direction.

She wasn't too happy about my comment and went into a rage. I couldn't believe how belligerent she became so fast. She leaped at me and would've knocked me down if Bishop hadn't gotten between us.

"Bitch, you don't need to be worrying about a ring. Worry about this ass kicking I am about to give you," she said, and then lunged at me again.

I ducked down and dodged the blow to my face. But when I came back up Keisha's left hand landed on the top of my head. Literally caught off guard, I lost my balance for a second, but after I regained control of my situation, I started swinging at everything around me.

"Bitch, you really fucked up now!" I roared as I threw some jabs in Keisha's direction. Unfortunately, none of my blows hit her. Two of my punches did, however, land on Bishop's back. He called himself trying to keep the confrontation to a minimum by getting between Keisha and me. I wasn't pleased at all, because Keisha got a chance to hit me in my fucking head and I wasn't able to retaliate the way I wanted. I instantly became livid and tried to move Bishop out of my way so I could get a clean shot at really hurting Keisha.

Keisha stood on the other side of Bishop, laughing at the fact that she snuck and punched me and I wasn't about to hit her back. To add insult to injury, she even threatened to do more harm to me. Her dumb-ass girlfriends stood on the sideline and laughed at me too.

Bishop was more livid than I was. "What the fuck is wrong with you, Keisha? Whatcha trying to get locked up? You know if the police find you in this mall fighting, they're going to haul your silly ass out of here in handcuffs," he spat.

"Fuck that! I'm tired of you disrespecting me with these bitches, Bishop. I keep telling you I'm gonna fuck up every chick I see you with," Keisha warned.

I burst into laughter. "I hope you don't think you did damage to me with that little-ass punch, bitch!" I commented sarcastically.

"Shut the fuck up, ho! You know I would bury your skanky ass!" she snapped. She acted like a crazy stalker. People who were shopping at the outlet walked by us and stared in disbelief.

"Yeah, whatever! Carry your fat ass on before I spit on you!" I snapped back, continuing to throw gas on the fire.

"Why don't you bring it on!" she screamed. "I swear I would beat the fucking breaks off you if I felt the slightest bit of your saliva hit me."

"Bring your fat ass back over here and I'll show you!" I roared. I had become fed up with this chick calling me names. She had literally gotten on my last nerve.

I must've gotten on her last nerve too because

like a thief in the night, she tried to sneak by Bishop to assault me again. But unfortunately for her, I was too fast for her slow ass. Bishop grew more furious and grabbed her by her right arm and forced her in the other direction. I heard Bishop yell a few times for me to close my mouth, but I ignored him. I wasn't about to let this fat bitch disrespect me and not put her ass in check. And besides, she hit me first. I hadn't laid one finger on her. I wished I had, but as life had it, she had one over me.

Meanwhile, Keisha's two friends stood around and acted like they wanted to attack me themselves. I watched them through my peripheral vision the entire time and waited for one of them to make the first move. Trust me, I wasn't in the mood to go head to head with those chicks, but I vowed to myself that if one of them approached me, then I'd have to bring the heat. Lucky for all the parties involved, they went their way and I did the same. And in the end, no one was hurt.

It took Bishop about fifteen long minutes to get Keisha under control. By the time he got back to me, I had taken a seat on one of the benches near the food court. I was not a happy camper when he approached me. My expression made him well aware of how frustrated I was about what just happened.

"Are you all right?" he asked.

As badly as I wanted to scream my lungs out for asking me that ridiculous question, I held on to what little composure I had left and forced myself to smile. Then I shook my head casually and said, "I did not sign up for all this drama. If I wanted to get into a fight, then I should've stayed in Virginia."

"Oh, so now it's my fault?" he asked me as he stood before me.

"Well, whose fault is it? Because the last thing I remember was, while I was walking alongside of you minding my fucking business, out of nowhere comes your big-ass girlfriend cursing me out and then she attacks me."

"Didn't I get between you two after she hit you?" Bishop defended himself.

"Yeah, but that was after she hit me upside my fucking head!" I snapped. At this point, I was angry as I could be. For him to stand there and act like he really saved the day was a fucking insult. If I was back in Virginia, I swear I would've told him to kiss my ass and walked off. But since I was here completely at his mercy, I found myself once again biting my tongue. I figured, why ruin my chances of staying here with him behind the dumb shit that had just happened with his fat-ass girlfriend? I also figured that if I acted like I was a bigger person than Keisha and that whole scene was water underneath the bridge, then I'd be able to score more points with Bishop and move Keisha's dumb ass out of the way. I mean, I did witness her say that she was tired of him disrespecting her with different women, so it makes me wonder how many women she's caught him with.

The only reason I could see Bishop cheating on her was because she was so fucking immature. I mean, come on, what grown-up starts fights with women she catches her man with? If anybody needs to be hit, it would be the damn man. It was apparent that Bishop was tired of Keisha's bullshit. And who knows, maybe I could be that woman who crashes her parade and ride off into the sunset with her man. I mean, Bishop was very easy on the eyes, not to mention he knew how to fuck me real good.

The only complaint I had regarding him was that he didn't get into the emotional part of the relationship.

He hadn't said he loved me, but that about sums it up. The kissing and touchy-feeling thing was off limits with Bishop. And that was cool with me, since he made up for it by keeping a roof over my head. So, what more could a girl ask for?

After I came to my senses, I let out a long sigh and then I stood up. "Ready to go?" I asked him.

He stood there and looked at me with the weirdest expression. I knew he wondered how I turned off the vexed button so fast and put on a happy face. My zodiac sign was Gemini, and we switch up like the weather. So, sooner than later, he'd get the picture.

"After you," he said, and then he waited for me to lead the way. So I walked off first.

"What's gonna happen if we walk out of this mall and she's waiting outside for me?"

"Don't worry. She won't be."

"What makes you so sure?" I wondered aloud.

"Because I made sure she left before I came back into the mall."

"If you say so," I commented, and then I headed toward the exit door on the east side of the mall. I hadn't expressed this to Bishop, but I liked the fact that I was the other woman. In my experience of being the side chick, I was always up for the challenge of moving the other chick out the way. Men I had dealt with in the past seemed to be more adventurous when they were hanging out with me. They could be whoever they wanted to be around me. They even spent more money to keep our relationship off the radar. I remember when I was with Duke, he gave me the fucking world. Nothing was off limits. And he spared no expense. Life was good until he flipped the script on me. From there, everything went downhill. Now I'm in another man's arms. And I'm sharing it with his main bitch, Keisha.

Being the main bitch meant that you were superior to all the bitches your man was fucking with. Unfortunately for Keisha, she didn't fit that bill.

In Bishop's case, it was clear after the way he handled Keisha, I knew I was only days away from stealing that bitch's title.

I'll take your man!

Chapter 2

Cock Blocking

After the mall incident, Bishop took me back to the apartment. During the course of the drive, we rode in silence. It was evident that he was extremely angry. The good thing about it was that I knew he wasn't at all angry with me. I struck up a conversation with him about his plans for later in the day, but when he acted a little apprehensive about answering my question, I left him alone and turned the volume up on the radio.

Not even five seconds after I turned up the volume, Bishop's iPhone rang. I knew deep down in my gut that it couldn't be anybody other than Keisha. She went to great lengths back at the mall to let me know that she wasn't going anywhere and that she would do whatever it took to get me out of the picture. So I figured I was about to be on the rockiest roller coaster ride of my life.

After Bishop answered his phone, I noticed that his mood changed drastically. He literally went from this angry guy to this mild-mannered gentleman. I even caught him smiling at one point in the conversation. I watched his every move through my peripheral vision. "When did you get in town?" he asked the caller, and then he fell silent for a brief moment. "Well, listen, after me and Torch make this quick run together, I'm gonna come see you. So be ready," he continued, and then he disconnected his call.

I was somewhat upset with the fact that he sat there and made arrangements to pay someone else a fucking visit while I was still trying to process what had happened earlier. I'd already made up my mind that I wouldn't nag him and I'd act as if everything was okay. But I still needed him to stick around and make me feel a little more secure than I was. I knew it had been only a couple of months, but I had fallen madly in love with Bishop, and I depended on him emotionally, mentally, and monetarily. So watching him spread himself thin between me, Keisha, and his everyday hustle had taken a toll on me. I had no one on my team but Bishop, and I'd be damned if I'd let someone else come between us.

After he pulled up in front of my apartment

building, I noticed he put the car in park and left the engine running. I knew this was my queue to take my ass into the house and find something to do while he took care of his business. "Are you coming back over here after you handle your business?" I asked him. I really wanted to know if he had plans to come back to see me tonight before he went home to Keisha's dumb ass.

He looked down at his watch and then he said, "Nah, I don't think I'm going to be able to come back tonight."

Disappointed, I sighed heavily and said, "Well, if you decide to change your mind, call me and let me know."

"A'ight," he replied, and then he gave me the look like he was waiting patiently for me to exit his car. So, without further hesitation, I opened the passenger side door and stepped down on the sidewalk next to the curb. Under normal circumstances, I'd kiss him before I got out of the car, but tonight I wasn't feeling the mood. And the fact that he didn't mention it led me to believe that he wasn't in the mood either. After I shut the door behind me, I said good-bye and then I walked toward my apartment building. I wanted to turn around and look back, but my pride wouldn't allow me to. I was that chick from Virginia, and back in VA we don't let the next person see us sweat. No way! That's not how we do things.

My apartment was on the first floor, and

you could see my front door from the street. So immediately after I got inside and sat my bags down on the floor, my doorbell rang. I knew it couldn't be Bishop, because he had a key and he would've let himself in. So, as curiosity reared its face, I made my way back to the front door and looked through the peephole. Unfortunately for me, I couldn't see through the damn hole. Someone on the outside literally had the hole covered with his or her finger or something. I was tempted to yell out and ask who was it, but for some crazy reason I couldn't get my mouth to open. So I stood there very quietly and said nothing. I even held my breath to prevent this unknown person from hearing anything on my side of the door.

The knocking continued while this person continued to cover the peephole. Sixty long seconds and one anxiety attack later, the person finally stopped knocking. But he or she insisted on leaving the peephole of my front door covered. I grew impatient and I figured that whoever was playing games wanted to remain anonymous until I opened the door. I became terrified that instant. I knew I needed to get Bishop on the phone immediately.

Very quietly I crept away from the door and headed toward the sofa, where I'd left my handbag, and I grabbed my BlackBerry. But as fate would have it, my BlackBerry started ringing as soon as I took it from my purse. Beyoncé's song "Countdown" started playing very loud. I fumbled with it, trying to stop the music from playing, because, for one, I wanted to mask the thought that someone was inside of the apartment. And two, I knew it was Bishop calling. He was the only person who had my number.

While I was pressing down on the send button to answer his call, the front door of my apartment was kicked open. The door slammed back against the wall behind it. The force of the kick caused the doorknob to punch a hole in the wall. I screamed, and my BlackBerry fell out of my hand, causing the battery pack from the back of it to fall out. I was standing in my apartment . . . alone . . . staring directly at two masked men. Both of them were at least six feet tall, and I could tell that they were black as soon as they opened their mouths. "Get down on the floor before I put a motherfucking slug in your head!" one guy roared.

I stood there paralyzed as I watched the other guy close the front door. "Bitch, didn't I tell you to get down on the motherfucking floor?" the same guy ordered as he rushed toward me. The manner in which he walked toward me gave me the impression that he meant business and if I didn't get down on the floor like he instructed me to, then I would pay the consequences.

So, without another moment of hesitation,

I fell down to my knees and leaned over to bury my face in the floor. My mind raced, trying to collect my thoughts. But the thought that dominated my mind was that my life had run its course. The writing was on the wall. The Carter brothers from Virginia had finally caught up with me to seek revenge for Duke's murder and any minute I'd be taking my last breath.

With that thought in mind, I immediately went straight into prayer mode. I hadn't talked to God since I'd asked him to help me escape from Katrina's house that night I jumped from the second-story window to prevent Duke from killing me. Now here I was right back in another deadly situation. I kept my eyes closed and asked God to forgive me for every possible sin I had committed. I even asked him to forgive me for getting into that rift with Keisha, even though she started all that drama. I mean, I couldn't afford to let anything keep me from getting into heaven after these guys pull the trigger.

While I was trying to get back in God's good graces, my would-be murderers were communicating back and forth with one another, and it caught me completely off guard.

"Where the fuck you going, nigga?" I heard one of the guys say in a strong Northeastern accent. It was very clear to me that he wasn't from the South. "Check the refrigerator and the freezer first, and if it isn't in there then go check the bedroom while I stay in here and watch her."

The instructions from one guy to the next immediately explained that they were here for something other than me, but what that something was I couldn't quite figure out. So I lay there in wait and prayed that whatever they were here for, they would hurry up and find it so they could leave. I also wished that they would leave me unharmed.

I lay there on the floor with my eyes shut, making sure I wasn't deemed as a threat to these guys. Unfortunately, my cooperation wasn't enough, because within seconds the guy who seemed to be in control gave his partner instructions to get me up. The other thug grabbed a fistful of my hair and pulled me to my feet. I stumbled a bit, trying to prevent this fucking maniac from pulling any of my hair out.

"Hey, wait! Ouchhhhh! You're gonna pull my hair out!" I yelled, on the verge of tears.

"Shut the fuck up, bitch, before I kill you right now."

It was hard, but I managed to calm myself in spite of the grip this asshole had on my hair. I swear I felt a few strands tearing from my scalp when he pulled me up from the floor. I tried to ease the pain by standing very close to him.

"Where the motherfucking money?" he asked me, sounding very frustrated.

"I don't know what you're talking about.

There's no money here," I told him, staring directly into his eyes, since that was the only visible thing on his face.

He wrapped his hand tighter around my hair and pulled me closer to him. My hair and the weave I had sewn in brought more pressure to my scalp after he tugged on them, causing my head to burn with excruciating pain. "Bitch, don't lie to me! We know Bishop keeps his stash here."

"I swear I'm not lying to you. If he got some money in here, then he never told me about it." I tried to plead with him as tears ran down my face.

The other guy came back into the living room where we were. "The refrigerator and the bedroom are clean. So there's gotta be another spot in here that I'm overlooking."

My captor yanked my hair yanked again and redirected my attention to the other guy. "Tell us where the money is, bitch!" he demanded. His tone sounded more terrifying with each word he uttered.

"I told you I don't know." I began to cry. The fact that I couldn't help them was a clear indication that they were going to end my life sooner rather than later. I really wished I knew what they were talking about, because I would've given it to them as soon as they entered the apartment. My life meant more to me than Bishop's stash. If you want to know the fucking truth, all the money in the world wasn't worth my life. How dare Bishop put me in harm's way like this. Evidently he did something to have these guys under the assumption that he hid his money in this apartment.

"I'm gonna give you one more chance to tell us where the money is. And if you don't, then your brains are going to be splattered all over the motherfucking floor," he roared.

Hearing this man tell me I was about to die if I didn't point him in the direction of Bishop's stash paralyzed me even more than before. I honestly wanted to kick myself for coming all the way up north only to end up in a fucked-up situation like this. I mean, I would've been better off getting killed back in Virginia. At least the few family members I dealt with from time to time would've been able to see that I had a proper burial.

"I'm gonna count to ten," he continued, and then he started counting down.

"One. Two. Three. Four. . . ." I heard him say, and then I tuned him out. I know I had to tell these guys something, but my mind wouldn't function. I even tried to think back to all the times Bishop came by with packages in his hands and went into different rooms in the apartment. Even with that information, my mind kept coming up blank. I didn't know what else to do but accept my fate. After I reiterated that I didn't know anything, I closed my eyes and waited for him to pull the trigger. When he got to ten, my tears soaked my face while I asked God to take my soul. Then I exhaled.

"Leave her alone. I can take it from here," I heard a familiar voice say.

I wanted to open my eyes, but I was afraid to for fear that my mind was playing tricks on me. Then I heard the voice again. "Y'all go ahead and leave. I'll catch up with y'all later."

When the voice resonated in my mind this time, I opened my eyes and turned in the direction it was coming from. I literally gasped for air when I saw Bishop standing at the front door. I could not wrap my mind around what was going on, especially after hearing him tell these fucking thugs to leave. I mean, why were they listening to him? Were they his friends or something? My mind was running full speed ahead as I watched both men exit the apartment. After Bishop closed the door behind them, he looked back at me.

I didn't know whether to hug him or curse him the hell out. I mean, what was that bullshit all about? Was that a test or something? I needed some answers and I needed them ASAP.

Bishop gave me this apologetic look as he walked toward me. But I refused to let him off the hook that easy. I was angry, and I felt like a complete fool. "I know you're mad right now. So, please let me explain," he began.

I tried to block out the throbbing and aching pain I felt in the back of my head, but

I couldn't. Bishop saw me massage the back of my head with my right hand, so as soon as he got within one feet of me he pulled me into his arms and started massaging my head himself. "I am so sorry, Lynise. But I had to let them take you through that, baby girl."

I pulled back from his chest and looked into his face. "But why? Whatcha don't trust me? I almost had a fucking nervous breakdown." I continued to sob.

"I know. I know," he said, trying to put my head back on his chest. But I resisted his efforts.

One part of me wanted him to hold me, but the other part of me wanted to curse him out. I felt so violated, and I wanted him to know it. "Bishop, I don't know what kind of game you're playing, but I don't like it. Those fucking monsters you had come in here and pretend that they were looking for some money you hid in here was a low blow to me. I mean, the way that guy handled me was wrong, and I am fucking pissed that you'd let him do that to me."

"You're right. But we're not in Virginia anymore. You're in my world now. Things are done a lot different here in New Jersey. I have a lot more at stake here, so I just needed to know if you were really down for me."

"I understand all of that, but haven't I proved who I was to you when we were back in

Virginia? I mean, that should've counted for something."

"Yeah, it did. But I still had to make sure," he insisted.

I wanted to sweep this misunderstanding underneath the rug, but my mind wouldn't let me. So I backed away from him and went into my bedroom. I needed to collect my thoughts, and I knew that I wouldn't be able to do it while I was in his arms.

Chapter 3

What Part of the
Game Is This?

After Bishop allowed those niggas to run me through the mill, I walked my ass into my bedroom and lay down so I could clear my head. Bishop came in the room behind me. I really wasn't in the mood to see his face, but at the same time I needed some comforting. My fucking head was aching and so was my entire body.

He sat down on the edge of the bed and began massaging my back. My eyes were closed as my mind drifted in thought. Everything from the events with Duke that happened back in Virginia to the fake robbery plot raced around in my head. The shit with Duke was still fresh on my mind and I was still fuming inside.

And then it hit me like a ton of bricks. Bishop was beginning to do the same underhanded tactics as Duke. Both men lived for the streets, they had women at home, and they made it known that they weren't answering to anyone. Not even me. To make matters worse, they'd cut you out of their lives at the drop of a dime.

I could sense that Bishop was still unsure about me. That thought was pretty upsetting to me. I was literally tired of running into niggas who didn't appreciate me. I had shit going for me. I was very attractive physically, and I wasn't stupid by a long shot. But more important, when I decided to be on your team, then you had my loyalty. So to keep getting the short end of the stick when I should have been given the whole enchilada had made me very resentful.

"Lynise, look at me," Bishop instructed. His tone was very gentle. He was somewhat different than the other assholes I had dealt with. He could be cool and gentle at times.

Lying in the fetal position, I turned and faced him while my head lay in a comfortable spot on the pillow. I didn't utter one word. I did, however, give him my undivided attention.

He cleared his throat and said, "Baby girl, my life here in New Jersey is very complicated.

I've got a lot of shit going on, and it's important that I have the right people around me that I can trust."

"First of all—" I began.

"Can you let me finish saying what I have to say?" Bishop cut me off midsentence.

"Sorry. I thought you were done," I replied nonchalantly.

"Well, I wasn't," he replied. "Like I was saying," he continued, "I've got several business ventures that are very important to me, so they require my full attention. I can't afford to have any slipups. So everyone around me has to go through certain tests or be eliminated."

Hearing Bishop tell me I had no choice in the matter was definitely a hard pill to swallow. At that moment, I realized I had just bit off more than I could chew. Bishop was on some mafia-type shit and I'd better get down with the program or keep it moving. One part of me wanted to ride or die with him, but the other part of me wanted to tell him to go to hell since I knew he had another bitch he took care of. But hell, I had nowhere to go, so I figured I would just sit still until a better opportunity presented itself.

After he fed me more reasons why he felt the need to have those niggas rough me up, he kissed me on the forehead and told me he was sorry. And finally after hearing something that made total sense, I felt good inside. Besides, the fact that he apologized, and the way he said it, sealed the deal. He looked sincere, and that's all I needed.

Once the air was clear between us, he instructed me to stay in bed and get some rest while he went into the living room to make a few phone calls. "I'm right in the next room if you need anything," he told me.

"Okay," I replied, and then I watched him leave the room and close the door behind him.

While I lay there trying to get some rest and hoping my headache would go away, I heard Bishop in the living room making small talk over the phone. It became obvious he was making business arrangements after I heard him give the caller instructions to have his money the following day. Bishop hadn't mentioned how much the person owed him, but his voice was stern, so it was understood that he was serious.

Immediately after he ended that call, he was making another one. This time his tone was different. He was in a better mood than before. In fact, it sounded like he was pleading for someone's mercy. Twenty seconds more into the conversation, I realized he was talking to Keisha. "Baby, why we gotta go through this?" I heard him say.

My whole mood turned for the worse. After being knocked around by Bishop's henchmen I was really not up for hearing him speak in that fashion. He was literally begging this bitch to cooperate with him and get with the program. In her heart I was sure she knew he was still with me.

"Whatcha mean why it's so quiet?" he questioned her. Then he said, "Look, I am not going to sit here and let you grill me like this. I am at my boy's crib trying to handle some business that may keep me out part of the night, so don't wait up for me."

After he lied to her about his whereabouts, he told her he loved her and then he told her good night. He was cool about the way he handled that situation . . . but I wasn't. I felt stupid to say the least. I mean, this guy really had his Mack game in full force.

And the more I pondered it, the more it made me think about how Duke played me. In the last days of my relationship with Duke, I felt robbed of my love, my trust betrayed. If I didn't learn much from that relationship with Duke, I did learn that niggas in the street didn't give a fuck about no one but themselves. I also learned that chicks like me come a dime a dozen and pussy was free. If I wanted to step outside that box from the other birds, then I needed to demand my respect.

While I continued to think about my position in life, I heard Bishop's BlackBerry ring. In a split second, a blink of the eye, I placed my thoughts on the back burner and zeroed in on his conversation. This time around, he kept his conversation to a minimum. Plus, he was speaking so quietly, it was damn near impossible to hear what he was saying. I did hear him tell the caller that right now wasn't a good time to talk and then he told them that he would call them back in a few minutes. This took me aback and I assumed he was talking to another chick on the phone. I mean, he never acted like that before. So I knew my suspicions had to be right.

Moments later he walked back into the bedroom. I was lying on my stomach with my face turned toward the wall and pretended to be asleep. I couldn't see what he was doing, but I felt the heat from his body when he loomed over me to see whether I had my eyes open. I thought he was going to call my name to see if I would answer, but he didn't. Seconds later, he walked back out of the bedroom and closed the door behind him.

Immediately after he closed the door, I opened my eyes and wondered what he was about to do. It didn't take long for me to get my answer; I heard Bishop open the front door of the apartment and then close it. When he left the apartment, my gut told me he was hiding something or someone from me. My mind was running rampant. At that moment I wanted answers. I didn't want to be left in the dark anymore. I was tired of his fucking secrets, and one of these days I was going to bring it to his attention. Right now, I was more interested in finding out whom he was talking to and what he was trying to prevent me from hearing.

I slid off the bed and made my way out of the bedroom. I peeped inside the bathroom and the other bedroom just to make sure Bishop wasn't playing another trick on me. When I was convinced he had left the apartment, I tip-toed down the hallway, and looked through the peephole. Just as I had expected, that son-of-a-bitch Bishop was standing on the opposite side of the door talking to someone other than Keisha.

I saw him laugh a couple of times, but I was unable to hear his conversation. I was pissed off about that too. I figured whoever it was on the other end of the phone made him happier than the two women he was fucking on his off days. The sight of him smiling from ear to ear like he had a huge crush on some hot new chick made me sick to my stomach. Men don't make other men smile like that unless they're gay. And since Bishop hadn't shown me any signs of him fucking another man, I assumed otherwise.

Something also told me that the person he was talking to probably knew about Keisha, but didn't know about me. Okay, granted, it was bad enough that I had to deal with him fucking Keisha. And yes, I was the one who came in town and rained on her parade. But still I wasn't about to let him bring another chick into the fold. I mean, come on, how many bitches does one man need?

I knew deep down in my heart that I needed to make my presence known. So I felt that the best way to do that was by catching him and the bitch on the phone off guard. Without further hesitation, I grabbed the doorknob, turned it quietly, and then pulled the door open. Bishop turned around and looked at me like a deer caught in the headlights. Before he had a chance to say another word to his mystery phone freak, I said, "Oh, I'm sorry, baby, I thought you were gone."

Bishop stood there speechless. The fact that I said *baby* loud enough for the new bitch to hear me made my motherfucking day. It felt as if I had scored a hundred points in a basketball game.

"What's wrong, baby? Are you all right?" I continued as I moved closer toward him.

"Oh, yeah, I'm cool," he finally replied while he gave me a cheesy-ass smile. And then without a moment's notice, he told the caller he would call them back and rushed to disconnect their call.

I was about a foot and a half away from Bishop when he hung up with the caller, so I couldn't hear their response. But I did hear a woman's voice, and I wasn't too happy about that. One part of me wanted to smack the shit out of him, but the other part of me wanted to act as if I didn't hear anything. My lack of bitching allowed him to stroke his ego, since that's what niggas like him do anyway.

"You didn't have to hang up the phone just because I came out here," I said, trying to act calm. When in reality I wanted to curse him the fuck out. I was sure he knew I had busted his ass with his hand in the cookie jar, but deciding not to react to his sneaky behavior threw him for a loop. I had his dumbass by the balls and he couldn't even see it.

"I'm kind of glad you came out here, because I've been trying to get that nigga off the phone for about five minutes now," he lied through his teeth.

"Who was it?" I questioned him. Seeing him squirm his way into a story full of lies was funny. I swear that whoever said men couldn't lie was truly on the money with that one.

"It was Monty." The lie flowed smoothly. "I owe him a favor and he called to collect on it. So I might have to go by his spot if he decides he doesn't want to come by here." Then he placed his arm around my shoulder and kissed me on the forehead. "And whatcha doing up anyway? I thought you were sleep."

"I was, but I had to use the bathroom, so I got up," I lied back to him. I figured since he wasn't being forthcoming, then why should I? I mean, at this point in our relationship, I felt like why be honest with him when he had more shit than the next nigga? And since he was proving to be just like Duke, I was gonna start looking out for number one. Which was me. Fuck that! I was tired of being the ride-or-die chick and a fucking punching bag for his friends to knock around when they wanted to prove a point. It was time for me to get what I could from this nigga while I could and then move on to the next best thing. I'd let Keisha and this new bitch battle it out.

Bishop escorted me back inside the apartment and tried to act like it was all about me by giving me a massage and telling me how he was lucky to have me in his life. I can't lie—everything he said sounded good, but it didn't mean shit to me. My mind had been made up about the way I looked at Bishop. This motherfucker was literally wasting his time.

Later that night, Bishop dozed off on the sofa in the living room while he was watching TV. It was a little after midnight, so I started to wake him and insist that he come in the bedroom to get in the bed. But when I heard his BlackBerry buzzing around on the floor near the sofa, curiosity struck me hard, so I snatched it up to see who was trying to contact him this time of the night. My first thought was that it had to be Keisha's dizzy ass trying to find out whether Bishop was staying with me, so I was ready to add fuel to the fire.

But when I looked at the caller ID and realized it was some chick named Chrissy, my heart sunk down into the pit of my stomach. Without thinking about it twice, I answered her call. I had to hear her voice if it was the last thing I did. Even though I pressed down on the send button to take her call, I had to tiptoe away from Bishop before I could utter one word. So, when I finally got halfway down the hallway, I whispered hello as if I had just awakened.

She hesitated for a second or two, so I assumed she was building up the nerve to open her mouth. Then she asked me if she could speak to Bishop.

"He's asleep. May I ask who's calling?" I replied, trying my best to remain cool. The last thing I wanted to do was to let this chick think that I was the least bit upset or jealous at the fact that she was calling Bishop's ass this time of the night. When you find out that your man has another bitch on the side, you gotta play the game with those hoes. You can't let them see you sweat. You've got to act as if you aren't fazed by them calling. If anything, play the role and be cordial, because, remember, bees are attracted to honey.

"Can you tell him Chrissy called?" she asked me.

"Sure. I can do that," I assured her.

"All right. Thank you."

"You're welcome," I said.

Then, as soon as I was about to disconnect our call, she interrupted me and said, "Excuse me."

"Yeah, what's up?" I asked.

"Um . . . never mind. Thank you," she replied, and then she hung up.

By the time our call ended, I was in my bedroom sitting on the edge of my bed. After I pressed the end button, I placed Bishop's cell phone next to me on the bed and wondered what the hell I got myself into this time around. At that moment, I really couldn't paint the full picture, but I knew it was a matter of time before I would be removing myself from this situation. And best believe that I would be compensated for my pain and suffering too. It didn't matter if I took it or he gave it to me freely. So, I guess, time would tell.

Chapter 4

In Over My Head

Later that morning, I was awakened by Bishop's numerous telephone conversations, and instead of getting up to start my day I lay there and eavesdropped. The first call I heard him make had to be Keisha, because he sure did a lot of explaining about why he hadn't answered his phone when she called. The second call he made I assumed was one of his employees, because I heard him literally spit fire through the receiver and threaten the person that if they hadn't taken care of what he instructed them to do, then it was going to be their ass on the chopping block. And during that conversation he also instructed that person to go back and make sure they did a thorough cleaning. "Yo, I swear, if that spot isn't squeaky clean, then we're gonna have some major fucking problems!" Bishop roared through the phone. "And the next time you wanna talk to me, don't call me on this phone, hit me up on the throw-away phone." he continued, and then he ended the call.

Several minutes later, I heard him make another phone call. But that call only lasted sixty seconds. And before I realized it, Bishop had burst into the bedroom and startled the hell out of me. He literally stood over top of me and screamed like his damn mind was going bad. I opened my eyes and saw the anger in his face.

"Haven't I told you not to answer my motherfucking phone?" he roared.

"Yeah, why?" I replied, knowing exactly where he was going with this conversation.

"Well, then, why the fuck you answered it while I was asleep last night?" he continued.

"I tried to wake you up," I lied. I needed a defense and I hoped that the lie I had just told would work. Unfortunately for me, it didn't. Bishop was not letting the matter go. He felt the need to chastise me because I caught his ass in the wrong. Not only that, it took the spotlight off him from the night before when I caught his ass standing outside the apartment talking and grinning from ear to ear with his new chick. But it was cool. I was a big girl, so I knew what to do for his ass.

"Look, Lynise, I don't give a fuck if I'm in a

coma, don't touch my cell phone anymore. Do you understand me?" he asked me.

"Yeah, I understand," I assured him.

Without saying another word, he stormed back out of the bedroom. And seconds later, I heard the front door open and then I heard it slam shut. "And fuck you too!" I mumbled.

Unable to go back to sleep after Bishop's tirade, I grabbed my BlackBerry from the nightstand and dialed Bria's number. I needed someone to talk to about Bishop's fucking anger issues. And who better to talk to than his sister, Bria. She knew him longer than I did, so there was no question in my mind that she could give me some pointers as to how to handle him the next time he goes on a rampage. Unfortunately she didn't answer her phone. I literally disconnected the call and dialed her number three times back to back, but still I got no answer. After the failed attempts to contact her, I sent her a text message and told her to call me when she got a chance. Immediately thereafter I got out of bed and went into the bathroom to take a shower. It didn't take me long to freshen up. I was in and out of the bathroom in a matter of ten minutes. I had nowhere to go, but Bishop had provided me with transportation a week after I had arrived in town.

To get out of the apartment, I decided to go out and get me a breakfast sandwich at one of the fast-food chains in the area. I slipped into a pair of denim booty shorts, a Hello Kitty tank top, and Nike flip-flops. After I brushed my hair back into a neat little ponytail, I grabbed my handbag and my car keys and headed outside.

On my way to my leased two-door silver Jaguar, my friendly neighbor, Sean, broke his neck to speak to me after he stepped out of his sky blue, big boy Chevy Tahoe. He was dark skinned and handsome like I like my men. Plus, he was the right height for me. He put me in the mind of Idris Elba. But he wasn't as fine as the actor.

I smiled and waved at him as I made my way toward my vehicle. Normally when we see each other, it's always in passing and Bishop is with me, so we would speak to each other and keep it moving. But for some reason I guess he wasn't trying to let me get out of his sight without saying a few words to me since Bishop was nowhere around.

I didn't know much about Sean except that he had just moved into the apartment three doors down from me a couple weeks ago. I hadn't seen too much foot traffic to his place since he had moved in, so I was forced to believe he was either single or gay.

He walked toward me with the biggest smile he could muster up. I looked at him from head to toe, and believe me, he looked really damn good rocking a pair of khaki cargo shorts, a white Lacoste polo, and a pair of brown signature Louis Vuitton sneakers. On the surface, he looked like he was a hustler. But after he opened his mouth, he gave me the impression that he was educated. He was intriguing to say the least.

"Leaving without me?" he said jokingly.

We both stopped and stood within a couple feet from each other. "It looks that way," I replied, and then I smiled.

"Where's your man?" he pressed on.

"Where's your woman?" I threw the question back at him.

"If I had one she'd be with me right now." He smiled. "But it's not about me, it's about you. So answer the question."

"I'm not sure. But I'm sure that wherever he is, he's fine."

"Well, where are you headed?"

"Out to get a breakfast sandwich. Why?"

"Maybe because I would like to tag along."

"I don't think my man would like me driving another man around in a car he's paying for."

"Oh, no, I was going to follow you in my truck."

I hesitated for a second and thought about Sean's offer. While the idea of our having breakfast together sounded good, the chances of Bishop or someone who knew him seeing us dining out in a restaurant didn't sit well with me. It would be disastrous.

Then after it dawned on me how Bishop was playing me with this new bitch named Chrissy, my whole perspective changed. Shit! Why not have breakfast with this handsome gentleman? It wasn't as if we're going to check into a hotel. One harmless breakfast date wasn't going to hurt anyone.

"Come on, let's go," I instructed him.

"Where are we going?" he wanted to know.

"To the nearest breakfast diner."

"Well, I know this spot on the other side of the city, so follow me," he insisted.

"Okay. Let's do it then," I replied, and then I headed to my car.

I followed Sean to an all-day breakfast spot called Tops Diner on Passaic Avenue. Immediately after he parked his truck, Sean rushed over to my car, opened the door, and held it open so I could step out. "Thank you," I said.

Minutes after we entered the diner we were seated at a table near a window. The restaurant wasn't busy, so we were able to get our food very quickly. I had chicken and waffles, while Sean dug into a Colorado omelet.

In the beginning, Sean and I made small talk. I gave him some of my backstory of where I was from and my educational background. When he asked me how Bishop and I met, I stretched the truth a bit. I told him Bishop and I met at a strip club back in Virginia, which was partially the truth. I failed to tell him Bishop only came to Virginia to avenge his brother's death and the real reason why I followed him to New Jersey. I was sure if I had told him about all the murder and mayhem that happened back in Virginia, he would've ended our breakfast date in the blink of an eye.

I had some bad history that no one needed to know about. And I wasn't stupid enough to share that kind of information. Even if Sean was the bad boy type, no way was I sharing information I had tucked in the back of my head and would carry to the grave. No one in their right mind would admit any wrongdoing or the fact that they were on the run from the police. So I continued to smile and act like I was Ms. Goody Two-shoes.

Halfway through breakfast Sean became flirtatious, and I loved every minute of it. After he told me he was twenty-nine years old with no kids and he had just graduated from Penn State, I was really impressed.

"So, what do you do for a living?" I pressed on.

He smiled shyly. "I'm kind of between jobs right now," he admitted.

"Well, how do you pay your bills?" I wanted to know.

Something inside of me told me Sean was slinging some type of narcotic. I always had an eye for a street hustler, and Sean had the look to a tee. And most often when a guy worked on the street, he had a certain mannerism. Meaning, he would cut his money with his back facing the person in front of him, he would talk in code while he was on the phone, and he would always look over his shoulder.

Since Sean and I had been eating, he had looked around checking out our surroundings at least ten times, if not more. That kind of behavior had drug dealer written all over it, but how was I to judge? I felt as if those were the only men I attracted, so I figured why fight it or try to change it.

Immediately after he told me that his parents were well-off and that they sent him money to pay his bills, I kind of took it with a grain of salt and said whatever. At that point it really didn't matter. I figured the less I knew about him, the better off I'd be. Besides, at the end of the day, how he got his money was his business, not mine.

"So, how many kids do you have running around here?" I asked him.

"One. I've got a seven-year-old son named after me."

"That's cool. Where is he?"

"He lives with his mother down South."

"Down South, where?"

"Atlanta, Georgia. His mother moved down there about a year ago to take care of her mother after her father passed."

"I'm sorry to hear that."

"Oh, it's cool."

"So, how often do you see your son?"

"Three to four times a year. But lately I've been able to see him more since I'm out of school now."

"How do you feel about him living so far away?"

"It doesn't bother me like it used to. They live in a really nice neighborhood and she's taking good care of him, so that's what really counts."

"How long have you and she been apart?"

"She and I separated right before my son's fifth birthday."

"Can I ask why?" I pressed the issue.

Sean smiled. "It wasn't anything huge. We just grew apart."

"Come on, now, be honest. You know you cheated on her."

Sean's smiled even harder. "I'm being honest," he tried to convince me. He continued to tell me about his past relationship with his son's mother, and then we switched gears and talked a little about my past relationship with Duke. To protect the guilty, which would be me, I refused to give him specific details pertaining to real names or the actual cities my ex-men resided in. I did, however, let the cat out the bag that Bishop had another woman and that I was the chick on the side.

Sean seemed very disappointed in me after I told him about the status of my relationship.

"Come on, I know you know that you're selling yourself short," he stated.

I didn't respond. I turned my head and looked out of the window.

He reached across the table and grabbed both of my hands. "Look at me," he instructed me. I turned my head back around to face him. "Are you happy?" he continued.

"What do you mean, like right now?"

"I'm talking about your situation with your man."

"I have my good days," I told him.

"Okay. But are you happy?"

I sat there and thought for a moment before I answered Sean's question. It didn't take me long to weigh the pros and the cons and discover that I really was not happy. But with everything looming over my head, I had to take what I got. Bishop may have been playing me, but he was keeping a roof over my head, lining my pockets with weekly allowances, and making monthly payments on my whip.

Where else could I get a nigga to pick up the tab for my living expenses? Nowhere. So, I might as well suck it up and deal with his bullshit before he replaced me like Duke did.

To close Sean's mouth, I lied and told him that I was fine and I had plans to leave Bishop high and dry once I got my act together. He acted as if he believed me, but then again one could never tell. Men sure know how to put on a facade when they need to. But let me be the first to say that women have mastered it. And that's some real shit!

Once we were done eating, he offered to take me to the 11:30 a.m. movie, but I declined. I lied and told him I had a hair appointment. As much as I wanted to go, my heart wouldn't allow me. I had to remind myself that I was living here in New Jersey on Bishop's tab. He had provided me everything I needed, so I had already played myself by accepting Sean's first date. And to accept an extended date would be blatant disrespect to Bishop. I knew it didn't seem like it, but I had some morals. So, after I thanked him for breakfast, I gave him a warm hug. And he returned the gesture with his cell phone number and then we went our separate ways.

When the cat's away the mouse will play!

Chapter 5

Is Blood Really Thicker Than Water?

From the time I got back into my car and until I drove about five miles, I could not get my mind off Sean. He was the perfect height, the right weight, the right complexion, and his choice of clothing was on point.

What more could a woman like me ask for when going out on a date?

In addition to his outer appearance, he drove a nice SUV and I could tell he had enough money to spread around. And what would seal the deal for him and me was if he had the balls to sweep me off my feet and snatch me right from under Bishop's nose. That would be some wicked shit! And if I found out his money was way longer than Bishop's, that would be even better. Oh, my God! That would be the ultimate bonus on my part. Time would only tell though.

Instead of going back to the apartment, I decided to go by the hair salon where Bishop's sister, Bria, worked. This was my way of finding something to do since there was a slim chance that I'd be able to spend time with Bishop. He left the apartment a couple of hours ago angry, so there was no telling when he'd return. Bria was the only associate I had outside of Bishop, so I utilized every waking moment she gave me.

Upon my arrival to the salon, I didn't see Bria's car parked outside. So I called her cell phone to see where she was, but to no avail. I disconnected the call on the fifth ring. I sat there in my car for a few minutes and then I tried to call her a second time. Still no answer. I debated whether I should go inside the salon to see if anyone knew where Bria was. But as fate had it, I didn't have to. Sarah, Bria's boss and the owner of the salon, came outside and headed toward her car.

"Hey, excuse me, Sarah, is Bria in the shop?" I yelled from inside my car.

She stopped in her tracks after I got her attention. Sarah was a very attractive Dominican chick. She sort of reminded me of

Jennifer Lopez with the body and all. She was a few years older than I was, but she didn't look it. "No, she's not here. And I haven't seen her in two days."

"Really," I said. "Well, if she happens to come in or call, let her know I came by."

"Okay. But if you talk to her before I do, tell her to call me," Sarah insisted.

"All right," I replied, and then I pulled off.

A couple of minutes into my drive away from the salon made me wish I'd taken Sean up on his offer to go with him to the movies. In a perfect world, things would go the way I wanted them to, but for some reason my luck superseded anything I put my heart and mind to. Karma was a bitch when it came to me. So I had learned to play the cards I was dealt.

I went back to my apartment, hoping I'd catch Sean so I could take him up on his movie date. To my surprise, he wasn't there. I was so devastated when I pulled up and didn't see his truck, I let out a long sigh and shook my head.

"Dammit!" I shouted as I punched the steering wheel with my fist.

I sat in the car for a few minutes, trying to figure out what to do. When I couldn't think of anywhere to go, I turned off the ignition and went into the apartment. I tossed my handbag and keys onto the coffee table and sat down on the sofa. Minutes after I laid my head back on the headrest, I grabbed the remote from the coffee table and turned on the TV. Nothing was playing that I was interested in watching, so I casually surfed through the channels and stumbled across my favorite music video on Black Entertainment Television.

I rocked my head back and forth to Jay Z and Kanye West's song "Niggas in Paris." I didn't know the words to the song, but acted as if I did. I became so engrossed in the song that I didn't hear the front door when it opened. I only realized Bishop had walked into the apartment after he shut the front door. He literally scared the hell out of me.

"Woooo, you scared me," I commented as I looked directly at him.

I noticed he wasn't wearing the same outfit he had on when he left the apartment this morning. I knew he had gone to the house he shared with Keisha and changed clothes. I started to make mention of it, but I changed my mind. I was too tired to go through another one of his screaming matches. I just wanted to relax and think about Sean.

"How long you been home?" he wanted to know.

"I just got back a few minutes ago," I told him while searching his face to see where this conversation was going. I also listened intently to the tone of his voice to determine what mood he was in.

He stood about three feet away from me and started asking me a series of questions. "Have you talked to Bria today?" he began.

"Nah, I haven't. I went by the salon to see her, but Sarah said she hasn't been to work in two days."

"Oh, that ain't unusual. Sometimes Bria won't go to work for days at a time," Bishop explained. "She's probably running behind that nigga she just started fucking with."

I started to comment, but I didn't. Bishop knew his sister better than I did. So I just allowed him to say whatever he wanted to. "How much gas is in the car?" he asked me.

"It's got a quarter tank."

"Well, get up 'cause I'm gonna need you to run to the store for me."

I rolled my eyes as I dragged myself off the sofa slowly, because I was not in the mood to go anywhere. Bishop saw my facial expression and had something to say. "Why the fuck you frowning?"

"I'm not frowning," I replied immediately.

"Then what do you call it?"

"Why are you trying to start an argument? Everything was fine before you came in here," I commented sarcastically.

"Don't forget that you're in here because I pay the motherfucking bills."

I sighed and totally disregarded his comment. I knew he paid the bills, so why should I add fuel to the fire? It was obvious he was still pissed off at me for answering his cell last night. It made me wonder about this Chrissy chick.

Anyway, to avoid an all-out war with him, I tried to diffuse the situation by asking him what he needed from the store. He gave me a list of five items that he wanted me to get. After he peeled off two twenty-dollar bills from the bank roll he had in his front pocket, I grabbed my things and headed back out the front door.

En route to the supermarket, I thought about Bishop's plot to send me on an errand run so he could be in the apartment alone. It bothered me that he didn't give me enough credit to know what's going on. Those asshole flunkies of his didn't burst into my apartment for nothing. Bishop's plan to scare the hell out of me was done to prepare me for what he had stashed at the apartment. He acted as if I never had a nigga in my life who didn't hustle and keep his dough stashed in a few hiding spots around the house. Quiet as it was kept, I had fucked more cats in my life that hustled in the streets than worked a nine-to-five. Hell, Bishop needed to get with the program.

The more I thought about it, I realized it would be kind of weird to fuck with a cat that had a legitimate job. How would I be able to steal money from his stash if he didn't have one in the first place? That would be a disaster, if you asked me. Chicks like me always needed a gangster, his money, a Taser for bitches like Keisha, and a get-out-of-jail-free card when shit started to pop off. If all of those things were in order, my life would probably run smoothly. Kind of run smoothly.

While I was at the checkout counter paying for the things Bishop asked me to get, my BlackBerry rang. I looked down at the caller ID and saw an unfamiliar number. It was a New Jersey area code. Although I had my doubts, I answered it. "Hello," I said. But the caller on the other end didn't say a word. It was dead silence. "Hello," I said once again. This time I heard a muffled noise, so I said hello for a third time. After getting no response, I disconnected the call.

Walking outside to the car I thought about the phone call I had just gotten. Curiosity tore me apart. I wanted to know who was on the other end, so I contemplated dialing the number back. When the possibility of it being Keisha's dumb ass came to mind, I knew not to waste my precious time. It wouldn't surprise me if she had gotten my number out of Bishop's cell phone this morning. I knew one thing—if I found out it was her, she and I were going to have some serious problems, and there wouldn't be a happy ending.

Back at the apartment, Bishop was nowhere in sight. I searched the entire place and I ended up with nothing. The thought of feeling stupid engulfed me, and I became livid instantly. The grocery bag containing his fucking cigarette lighter, sandwich bags, baking soda, a two-liter Pepsi, and plastic cups was tossed on the kitchen table the moment I entered the kitchen. I couldn't hold my composure. I had to call Bishop and blast his ass for sending me on a dummy run to the fucking supermarket to get him some shit he didn't need and then leaving before I got back. What kind of inconsiderate shit was that?

I wasted no time getting Bishop's ass on the phone. His phone rang twice before he answered it. "What's up?" he said.

I didn't want to come off strong or cause an argument, but I knew my tone had to be stern. I needed to let him know that I didn't appreciate the way he played me. "Are you coming back to the house?" I asked him.

"Yeah, later. Why?"

"Because you sent me to the store to get those things you had on the list, but when I came back you weren't even here," I replied. I sighed so he'd know that I was more frustrated than angry.

"I had to make a quick run. But I'll be back as soon as I can," he replied nonchalantly.

"Yeah, a'ight," I said as I ended the call.

I stormed out of the kitchen after I hung up with Bishop. The fact that he had no regard for my feelings made my blood boil, and I felt the need to do some more snooping. There was something he was trying to hide from me, and the only two things that came to mind were money and dope. Bishop didn't know me that well. I was going to find out which one it was.

The first place I searched was the bathroom. I took the lid off the back of the toilet, I looked underneath the sink in the bathroom, I searched through all the contents of the cosmetic drawers, and then I looked through the dirty clothes hamper. Shit, nothing. I found absolutely nothing.

The next place I searched was the hall closet. Bishop had a few boxes of his things stacked on top of each other, but I didn't touch them. I could tell he hadn't moved them. I could also tell he hadn't moved the two storage containers on the shelf, and since I knew there weren't any secret storage places inside the closet I closed the door and headed into my bedroom.

From the moment I crossed the threshold into my room, I could tell that Bishop had been in there. The mattress on my bed was moved. I knew because the flat sheet was no longer tucked completely between the mattress and box spring. I learned in jail how to make and tuck your sheets the way the military does, which was exactly the way I had it before I left the apartment. I rushed over to that side of the bed and struggled to lift up the king-size mattress. I grunted with the effort to hold up the mattress while looking to see if Bishop hid money or dope underneath.

When I realized he hadn't, I let that heavy-ass mattress go and watched it as it flopped back down on the box spring. I was breathing really hard because I was tired. That mattress was heavier than I'd thought. But that didn't stop me from continuing my search. I stood by the bed and wondered why the mattress was moved when there was nothing out of place but the sheets. Then it hit me. Bishop wanted me to find the bed messed up to throw me off track. I kind of smiled inside. That motherfucker didn't trust me, and that was cool with me. I wasn't going to disappoint him. So I continued my search.

I began to look around the room. I noticed that my perfume bottles on the dresser were moved. I always positioned them three inches apart from each other, and I made sure all the bottles were faced forward. Now they weren't the way I left them. I rushed toward my dresser because the only reason Bishop would have to rearrange my perfume bottles was if they fell down. And the only reason they would fall down was because he opened up one of the three drawers on the right side.

I didn't waste another second as I opened the top dresser drawer that stored my socks and footies and noticed he hadn't tried to hide anything in there. Next, I opened the second drawer with all my bras and panties and realized he hadn't hid any money or drugs in there either. I figured my bottom drawer might be the hideaway spot I was looking for, because it stored all my lingerie and I had a lot of that.

Before I opened up the last dresser drawer, I noticed my heart was beating faster than normal. I couldn't tell you whether it was my adrenaline rushing or because I feared the possibility of Bishop walking in and catching me looking for his stuff. Whatever it was, I knew I needed to get a handle on it and take care of my business.

"Come on, Lynise, let's find Bishop's stash," I said out loud to give myself that extra push. I needed the self-motivation.

Immediately after I pulled the drawer open, I noticed that none of my lingerie had been moved and I was completely bummed out. I was disappointed when I realized I'd hit yet another brick wall.

I sat back on my legs and racked my brain trying to figure out whether Bishop sent me out of the apartment so he could hide his shit. And if that was the case, where in the hell was it?

Frustrated by walking into another dead end, I pushed the drawer back in place, and to my surprise it wouldn't go all the way back in. What the hell? The light popped on in my head. Immediately I knew something was keeping me from shutting the drawer properly, and it had to be something that Bishop had placed there.

I pulled the drawer back out, and when it was completely pulled out, I was stunned to find a gray package taped to the bottom. The package was half the size of an iPad, but it was thick in width, which explained why it jammed the drawer when I tried to push it back in place. With the entire drawer in my hand I leaned down to smell it, but the scent was completely blocked. Whoever wrapped this thing up definitely knew what he was doing.

Since I had nothing to go on but assumptions, I figured it couldn't be anything else but a block of heroin or coke. I wanted to pry it open to see exactly what it was, but I didn't think I'd be able to wrap it back up the way that I found it. So I left well enough alone. Either way I looked at it, it was worth a pretty penny.

I continued to inspect the package when all of a sudden the doorbell rang. I nearly jumped out of my damn skin. I didn't know whether to put the drawer back or ignore whoever was at the door. But when the doorbell rang two more times, my heart fell into the pit of my stomach as I shoved the drawer back into the dresser and stood on my feet.

"Oh, my God! Who could that be?" I mumbled underneath my breath as I tried to make sense of what was going on around me.

"Oh, my God! It could be the fucking police coming in here to raid the place." I panicked. "I swear, I can't lie down and let them lock me up behind another nigga's dope. Hell, naw! I can't let it go down like that. And especially after the way he's been treating me lately. I'd be a damn fool." I don't know why I was tripping or why I went in panic mode. I was hoping to calm down as I tiptoed my way toward the front door.

DING! DONG! DING! DONG! chimed the doorbell. Whoever it was on the other side of the door made it pretty obvious that they weren't leaving until I answered. My heart rate continued to climb with each second that passed. And then the unexpected happened. "Lynise, open the door. It's me, Sean," I heard the familiar voice yell out.

Relieved that it wasn't Bishop or the cops trying to come in, I raced toward the door with a newfound sense of joy. Hearing Sean's voice felt like a weight had been lifted off my shoulders. From the moment I opened the front door everything seemed blissful.

"What took you so long to answer the door?" he wanted to know.

"And who gave you the balls to ring my doorbell? Do you know you're playing with fire?" I commented.

"If you're talking about your man, I saw him when he hopped into his ride and jetted down the block about five minutes before you came back."

"Don't let me find out you're a stalker," I joked.

He smiled and said, "I'm far from that. But if I see something I like and want, I've gotta make sure the coast is clear."

I giggled. "That's really cute," I replied bashfully.

"Not as cute as you are," he commented.

I smiled. "Cut to the chase. What's up?"

"I came over here to see if you'll go to dinner with me tonight, since you didn't accept my movie date."

"Can you give me some time to think about it?"

"How much time do you need?"

"Not long. I'll let you know within the next hour or so."

"Well, do that. And don't keep me waiting."

"I won't. Now, hurry up and get back over to

your spot before Bishop pulls up and catches you over here."

Sean looked over his shoulder and then he cracked a smile. "Trust me, I'm not worried about him," he commented as he walked off.

I'm playing with fire!

Chapter 6

I Need More Proof

Relentlessly thinking of ways to catch Bishop with his pants down gave me an appetite, so I took Sean up on his dinner offer. But it was only under the condition that we drove in separate cars. He agreed, and so it was settled. I wanted to change into something more casual, but with a sexy twist. However, I decided against it. I would have had a lot of explaining to do to Bishop if he came back to the apartment and waited for me to return, only to see that I changed attire. It would be World War III up in this apartment. And I wasn't in the mood for any of that drama.

It was Sean's idea for us to dine at this Italian restaurant about twenty miles across town. It was also his idea to select our entrée. I thought it was romantic and gave him the green light. The waiter poured us glasses of red wine while Sean started a warm conversation with me.

I looked at him closely as he told me how long it had been since he had been in a serious relationship. The way he licked his lips and looked me directly in the eyes spoke volumes to me. I was sure this was his normal way of communicating with women, but there was something else about him. I couldn't quite put my fingers on it, but I vowed to figure it out before the night was over.

While he and I talked, my BlackBerry rang. I looked down at the caller ID, but the number was blocked, so I ignored the call and pressed the end button. Several seconds passed and my phone rang again. I figured it was the same caller, because the number was blocked again.

"Sounds like someone is really trying to contact you," Sean commented.

"They don't want to get in contact with me that bad by blocking their number," I replied.

"Maybe they don't know their number is being blocked. I saw on TV that some cell phones do that because of minor glitches in cell phone towers."

I thought about what Sean said, but by the time it registered, my phone stopped ringing. "Oh well, I guess I'll never know who it was," I commented, and before I stuffed my BlacBberry back into my handbag, it started ringing again.

Sean smiled. "I see they're not giving up."

I smiled back and then I pressed the send button and placed the phone next to my ear. "Hello," I said.

"Help me," the voice said. It was barely audible.

I became alarmed by the woman's voice. "What did you say?" I asked, hoping I could get a clear understanding of what I had just heard. "Who is this?" I continued, also hoping the caller would identify herself. Unfortunately, the call was disconnected.

Immediately panic-stricken, I held my phone in my hand and looked directly at Sean, who by this time had started eating his food.

"What happened?" he asked after swallowing.

"I'm not sure," I began to explain. "Right after I said hello, I heard a woman's voice say 'Help me.' But when I asked her who she was, the phone hung up."

"If you sat back and thought about it, do you think you'd be able to recognize her voice if you heard it again?"

"I'm not sure," I said, as I began to wrap my mind around the entire phone call. The thought of someone calling me and asking me to help them and then hanging up was rather spooky.

"Can you think of anyone you know that could possibly be in trouble?" Sean pressed the issue.

"No, not really. I mean, I've only had this

number since I've been here in Jersey, and the only people who have it is the guy I mess with who put me in that place, a couple of boys that work for him, and his sister. Other than that, I couldn't really say."

"So you don't have any female friends here in New Jersey except for your boyfriend's sister?"

"No. I really don't," I acknowledged, and then I fell in deep thought.

"What's on your mind?" he asked me.

"I hope I'm not putting too much into what I'm about to say, but I haven't spoken to his sister in a couple days now, and when I went by the salon earlier, the lady she works for said she hadn't been to work in two days. So what if that was her on the phone asking me to help her?"

"Hold up. Let's not jump to conclusions. There's probably a good explanation why his sister isn't at work. For all we know she could be out of town or hanging out with her boyfriend."

I let out a long sigh. "I don't know, Sean. Something just ain't right."

"What do you mean?"

"I just remember that I got the same call earlier. But whoever it was didn't say anything. I said hello about two or three times and they didn't say anything. So I hung up."

"It's probably just someone pranking you."

"I hope so," I said, and then I tried to block

the whole incident out of my head so I could enjoy the rest of my date.

As the night ended and Sean and I stood in the parking lot of the restaurant near our cars, Bishop made it his business to get me on the line. I answered his call while Sean stood next to me. "Hello," I answered.

"Where the hell you at?" he didn't hesitate to ask.

"I ran out to get myself something to eat. But I'll be back at the house in about thirty minutes."

"Yeah, a'ight," he said, and then he hung up before I could utter another word.

After Bishop hung up on me, I casually dropped my phone back into my handbag and then I turned my focus to Sean. "I take it he summoned you to get back to the apartment."

"Something like that," I responded nonchalantly.

Sean extended his arms. "Can I get a hug before you leave?" he asked.

I extended my arms and stepped toward him, but then I stopped in my tracks. "Oh, naw. I can't do that."

"You can't give me a hug?"

"No. Because your cologne may get on my clothes and I wouldn't know how to explain my way out of that one."

"Well, can I give you a kiss on the cheek?"

"Sure. Why not?"

Sean leaned toward me and planted his semi-wet, soft lips on my left cheek. When he pulled back from my face we looked at one another and smiled. "Maybe next time I'll give you some lip action," I commented.

"That would be nice," he replied.

He watched me get in the car and waited for me to pull out of the parking lot before he got into his SUV. I blew him a kiss and made my exit. As I drove away I checked him out through my rearview mirror and noticed how quickly he grabbed his cell phone from his pocket and placed it up to his ear.

That move definitely raised a red flag for me. And it led me to believe he had to check in with his woman, despite the fact he claimed not to have one. The more I thought about it, the more turned off I was getting.

Okay, granted, I was supposed to be fucking with Bishop. But guess what? I made that known from the very beginning. But I really couldn't say the same about Sean. And as I thought back on dinner, his phone hadn't rung the entire time he and I hung out together, which was probably because he had it powered off.

Realizing this placed a nasty taste in my mouth. "Niggas are always talking about how much they keep it real when they're lying the entire time," I uttered, and then I shook my head in pure disgust. I was pissed that I was risking what little security I had with Bishop for a bitch-ass nigga like Sean. This so-called dinner date was a bad idea.

The radio took my mind off my bad move for a minute. During my drive I came up with a good story to tell Bishop if he asked me how long I had been gone and where exactly I was. Oh yeah, I had my lie mapped out to a tee. I figured lying to him wouldn't do our relationship much harm since he started lying to me first. And in the end, things would play themselves out the way they supposed to. That's called divine nature. And no one escapes that. Not even me.

What's yours is yours!

Chapter 7

Method to the Madness

Bishop, Monty, and Torch were sitting in the living room when I walked into the apartment. My heart kind of fluttered when everyone's attention turned toward me. My first reaction was to run, but Bishop told me to come in and close the door. I felt a little at ease because his tone was somewhat calm.

I stepped completely into the apartment and closed the door behind me like I was instructed, but I didn't move too far from it. "What's going on?" I asked, still standing within arm's length of the front door, holding a McDonald's bag in my hand I had just picked up.

"Remember when you told me you went looking for Bria at the shop earlier?" Bishop spoke first.

"Yeah, why?" I asked as my heart began to pick up speed.

"We think she's gone missing."

"Get the fuck out of here! You can't be serious!" I blurted out.

"No, I'm serious. And we think it's the niggas that I got a beef with across town who kidnapped her."

My heart stopped cold and collapsed in the pit of my stomach. I wasn't nearly as close to Bria as Bishop was, but the thought of her being kidnapped and possibly hurt was gutwrenching. And what if it had been me? The way those niggas snatched Bria up could very well have been the same way they'd gotten me.

"Oh, my God! I got two calls today, and it was probably her trying to tell me where she was at," I announced to everyone in the room.

Bishop sat up on the sofa. "When did that happen?" he asked me.

Wanting to help him as much as I could, I rushed over to him and showed him in my call log the two calls I received hours apart from one another. "If this was her, this was the first time she called me," I began to explain. "But for some reason she didn't say anything. And then we got disconnected. And this was the second time she called. And when I said hello, I heard a woman whisper, 'Help me,' and when I asked her to repeat herself, the phone hung up again."

"Did you hear any noise in the background?" Bishop asked me.

"No, I didn't hear anything. It was completely quiet."

"Why didn't you tell me this before?"

"Because it didn't dawn on me that it could've been her."

Looking a little frustrated, Bishop got up from the sofa and walked into the kitchen. I turned around and watched him leave. Several seconds after he walked into the kitchen, he turned back around and reentered the living room. "Are you sure you didn't hear any background noise?" he wanted to know.

"Yes, I'm sure. All I heard was when she said 'Help me.'"

Bishop started pacing from the kitchen to the living room. It was evident that he was trying to devise a plan, the details of which he kept quiet.

I couldn't stand being in the dark, so I asked him, "Do you know how long they've had her?"

"As far as we know, they scooped her up two nights ago after she left the shop."

"How do you know that?" I continued my inquiry.

"I've got my sources."

"Well, did your sources tell you where she was taken?" I could understand that he was under a lot of stress, but so was I. Hearing about the kidnapping of a woman whom you had close ties to was scary.

"Do you think we would be having this conversation if I knew where she was?" he replied sarcastically.

"Well, don't bite my fucking head off. I'm only trying to help."

"You can help me by staying out of my way. I've got everything under control," Bishop snapped.

Taken aback by his disrespectful behavior, I wanted to curse him out, but instead of choosing that way, I threw my hands up and went into my bedroom. After I closed my bedroom door, I stood next to it to eavesdrop on Bishop's conversation with Monty and Torch. I heard all three of them talking amongst themselves, but I couldn't decipher a word they were saying, so I acted as if I had to use the bathroom and walked back into the hallway. It shocked me that the living room went completely silent the moment I came back out of my bedroom. Noticing this gave me an uneasy feeling, so I went straight into the bathroom and closed the door behind me.

While I was washing my hands, Bishop knocked on the door and told me he was about to leave. I rushed to dry my hands with one of my decorated bathroom towels, and I opened the door before he walked away from it.

"So you're gonna leave me here by myself?" I asked as he stood before me.

"Don't worry, you'll be fine. Nobody knows where this apartment is," he assured me.

I kind of believed him, because why else would he hide his dope here? Cats in the game only stashed their money and drugs in spots where people would least expect or had no knowledge of. Because of this, I started to feel just a tad bit better.

"Are you coming back?" I asked him.

"I'm not sure."

"Well, would you at least call to check on me every so often?" I damn near pleaded.

"Yeah, I'll call you when I can," he said.

Before he walked away I leaned toward him, and he kissed me and said good-bye. I followed him along with Torch and Monty to the front door and watched them as they left. After they hopped into Bishop's vehicle, I closed the front door and locked it.

I tried to cope with the fact that Bria had been kidnapped and that she tried to call me, but my mind wouldn't allow me to come to grips with it. The thought of someone hurting her gave me chills. I didn't care how or why she was kidnapped; I just knew that she didn't deserve any of this. So I hoped that Bishop and his crew got to her before something tragic happened.

I swear I was mentally worn out. I was so

tired of placing myself in the middle of violence. Damn, I actually felt like a violence magnet. I couldn't get away from the shit. *Can't we just all get along?*

I knew if Bishop came back and told me Bria was found dead, I'd flip out and cry my heart out first and then I'd catch the next bus out and head west. The next time anyone would see me would be in the afterlife, sipping on a blue martini with an orange slice garnish on the side of my glass. I figured that life would be better than the one I lived in now. Between the bitches I deemed friends and the niggas that called themselves my man, I struck out every time I swung at bat. Now, how fucked up was that? If my mom would've played the mommy role in my life, I knew I wouldn't be here.

Life is a BITCH!

Chapter 8

America's Most Wanted

Several hours after Bishop left, I got in bed and tossed and turned all night. The different sounds I heard outside of my bedroom window had me somewhat on edge. At one point I thought there was someone inside the apartment, but when I got up to investigate, I realized I was the only one there. Relieved that I was just hearing imaginary sounds, I was able to get back in bed and fall asleep.

The following morning I woke up around nine and immediately zoomed in on my Black-Berry and noticed Bishop hadn't called while I was asleep. A little worried because I hadn't spoken to him since last night, I called him. To my surprise, Keisha answered his phone.

"Bitch, you ain't got enough of fucking with my man, huh?" she spat.

Hearing Keisha's rant coming through the phone made me cringe. I had called to check on Bishop and to find out the status of Bria, but got this bitch on the phone instead. I swear she had barked up the wrong fucking tree this time, and I unleashed my wrath with vengeance. "You got a motherfucking nerve, you fat bitch!" I roared. "Why do you insist on thinking Bishop is your man? He's my man, you slut bucket! He came all the way down south to pick me up and brought me back to his hometown so we could be together. Now, shouldn't that tell you that he's my mother-fucking man?"

"Listen, you fucking ho! Bishop and I got history, so I wouldn't let you or any other gutter-ass bitch jeopardize that!" she snapped.

"Bitch, please! He and I are already making plans to leave this fucked-up ass place and head out West." I laughed in her ear. I wanted her to hear the humor in my voice, so she would know I wasn't fazed by her threats. I also had to show her that I was in a better position to walk away with Bishop. I was more of a thorough bitch than she was. All she wanted to do was sit around and eat herself to death and try to scare off every chick that Bishop brought into his life. Evidently, he was tired of her fat ass. Why else would he put me up in a place, pay all my bills, put me in a car, and give me an allowance once a week? Okay, granted, he had been acting kind of shitty these last few days. But with all the stress and demands he had on a daily basis he's entitled to have mood swings. I just wished he wouldn't take his frustrations out on me anymore.

"Why the fuck you answered my phone? And who the hell you talking to?" I heard Bishop roar in the background.

"It's that dumb bitch you had with you at the mall!" Keisha yelled.

"Give me my motherfucking phone!" Bishop snapped, and then I heard a little scuffle noise. Seconds later, the line disconnected.

Shocked at what had just gone down between Keisha and Bishop, I stood there with my BlackBerry in hand and waited for him to call me back. I waited for three minutes, and when my phone hadn't rung, I called him back. Unfortunately, his line wouldn't ring. It went directly to voice mail. After trying to reach him four more times, back to back, I gave up.

It took me about ten minutes to get over that argument I had with Keisha's dumb ass. I swear, if I was standing in front of her when she started popping off at the mouth like she did over the phone, I would've spit on that bitch instantly. I thought I hated Diamond's guts, but Keisha definitely put a new meaning to the word *hate*. I seriously hated her, and when I hate someone, I can cause some serious damage to their asses. I knew one thing, Keisha better stay away from me or she'll find herself pushing up daisies like Diamond's and Duke's dumb asses.

Aside from all the drama Keisha caused, I was able to hear Bishop's voice in the background. But the downside to this was that I wasn't able to speak to him and find out about Bria. I really hoped he had a chance to either get her back or find a way to make things right with the other guys. Maybe they would let her go peacefully. In my book, money solved a lot of problems. In the world Bishop navigated, money was power and spoke volumes. So maybe he'd be able to make a reasonable exchange with a feasible ransom.

Over three hours passed and I still hadn't heard from Bishop. I tried to contact him once more, but with no success. I figured he'd answer my call since he knew Keisha and I had gotten into a heated argument. But once again, his phone went directly to voice mail. Irritated. That was me, and that was putting it lightly. I had no control over everything that was going on around me. It was fucking with me. Not knowing, not being able to find anything out, was disturbing. And the unknown was, if they could grab Bria, it only made sense that they could grab me as well.

I decided to leave the apartment and go out to Starbucks to get me a caffeine fix. Plus,

I needed to calm the fuck down and get some perspective.

Before I left the apartment, I was curious to know if Bishop moved the dope package from underneath my bottom drawer. To my surprise, it hadn't been moved at all. So I put the drawer back in place, ensuring it was closed tight.

I slipped into another one of my favorite white tees and a pair of sweatpants and then I made my exit.

I felt it was best that I clear my mind and think of how I could help Bria without putting myself in harm's way. Quiet as it was kept, Bishop needed some help. If he hadn't found the location of his sister by now, then he could forget about finding her alive. The way niggas were nowadays, they killed anyone who got in their way. And I was definitely not trying to be one of them.

While I was out making my Starbucks run, I had to stop at the nearest gas station to fill up or else I would be walking back to the house. There was a BP service station two and a half miles from the apartment, so I pulled up to the first pump. I didn't have a debit card to pay at the pump, so I went inside and paid the male attendant behind the fiberglass window. After I gave him forty bucks he handed me a gas receipt and then I left the store.

While I pumped the gas, a familiar SUV pulled into the service station and parked directly next to me. My heart started beating a little faster than normal. I had to admit, Sean had something to do with it.

He rolled down the driver-side window and asked me if he could pump my gas for me.

"I can manage it," I assured him.

"Where you on your way to?" he asked me.

"Has anyone told you that you ask too many damn questions?" I asked him, and then I turned my attention back toward the pump.

He smiled. "All the time."

I kept my head turned away.

"Had breakfast yet?" he continued.

"Have you?" I replied sarcastically, as if I was implying something.

"No, as a matter of fact I haven't. And if you like, we can head back over to our spot," he offered.

I had reached my price limit for my gas, shook the hose a couple of times to get every drop of gasoline in my tank, and when I was done I pulled down the lever and placed the hose back on the hook. I then twisted the cap back on the gas tank and closed the cover.

I looked at Sean. The man was very handsome and well manicured. It was something about his smile that sent chills through me. The initial interactions I have with men are always stimulating. They always put on their best smile and charm just to woo me, and then after they get the pussy, they start to show their true colors. I wondered if I gave Sean the time of day, would he play me like Duke did or treat me the way Bishop was treating me? It was a tough call, but time would tell.

"Why don't you call your girlfriend and ask her to meet you for breakfast?" I finally said. I couldn't hold my tongue back. I had to let him know I saw him making a call while I drove away from the restaurant last night.

"I told you I don't have a girlfriend."

"Well, who were you talking to after I left you standing in the parking lot last night?"

"It wasn't a girlfriend," he said adamantly.

I let out a chuckle to let him know I didn't believe a word he said. But I wasn't through with him. I had to press the issue, but I figured if I used reverse psychology he'd feel comfortable enough to spill the beans and tell me the truth about his love life.

"Look, you and I just met, so you don't have to lie to me," I told him. "If you have a woman, that's cool. I mean, it would be nice to warn me just in case she saw us together."

I stood near the driver's side of the car and waited for him to come clean with me. But unfortunately, he didn't budge. "Trust me, if I had a girl in my life I would tell you. But I don't," he said.

I was utterly turned off by Sean. I would've hung out with him in a heartbeat. But I couldn't be around a nigga I couldn't trust. I know Bishop hadn't been trustworthy lately, but at least he was paying the fucking bills. Sean, on the other hand, had just come on the scene and he was messing up already. It was time to give his ass the finger. I opened my car door and said, "With all the shit I got going on in my life, I ain't got time for you and your lies. So, please kick rocks!"

Immediately after I got back into the car, I revved up the engine and tried to pull off, but Sean pulled his truck in front of me, preventing me from leaving. So I put the car in reverse and tried to back up, but a black Suburban with smoke-tinted windows pulled up behind me and blocked me in. I was about to jump out of my fucking skin from mere fright. All I could think was that I was about to be the next kidnapped victim and Sean was behind it.

My heart was doing somersaults underneath my chest cavity as it pumped with fear. When I saw Sean hop out his driver's seat and reach for the handle of my passenger's side door, I panicked and locked it before he could open it. I wasn't about to let him or the other guys in the truck behind me take me away without a fight. Since I had nothing in my possession to help me fight these guys off, I grabbed my cell phone from my purse so I could call Bishop and tell him where I was and what was going on so he could help me.

Immediately after Sean saw me with my phone in my hand, he jumped across the hood of the car and begged me not to make that call. Then he pulled out a two-sided ID holder with a badge on one side and an ID card on the other side, and pressed it against the driver's side window.

"Lynise, I am an FBI agent. Your life is in danger, so please do not make that call," he begged me.

What the fuck? Shocked, more or less, I didn't know what to say or how to react after he flashed his badge in front of me. At first sight, I didn't know if it was fake and if this was one of his tactics to keep me from calling Bishop and to get me out of the car. But when the other two men stepped out of the SUV behind me, I saw they were white. They too flashed their FBI badges.

Something told me they weren't the cats that had a beef with Bishop and kidnapped Bria. Somewhat convinced that Sean and his cohorts were the real thing, I finally stepped out of the car. For the first time, I could honestly say that when I stood before him, I was completely at a loss for words. After he showed me his badge, I didn't know whether to address him as Sean or agent. But I knew that things would be different between us from this day forward. Something else I had to deal with.

I waited for him to tell me that he and the other two agents were there to escort me back to Virginia. I knew this was about those murders involving Diamond, Duke, and Katrina. But when he told me he was there to talk about Bria, my mouth fell wide open.

"Well, since you know I'm a federal agent now, I guess it's safe to tell you that I'm Agent Sean Foster and these two guys are Agents Morris and Paxton." Sean formally introduced himself and his fellow agents. "We were assigned to work the Ronsdale case with Bishop as the ring leader. When his sister, Bria, was busted on drug charges and money laundering, we made her a deal that if she helped bring down her brother and his lieutenants by wearing a wire and secretly recording their conversations, then she wouldn't do one day in jail.

"But the night before she was supposed to appear in front of a grand jury with the information to help us secure federal indictments for Bishop and the other men in his organization, she vanished. And we believe Bishop had something to do with it."

Trying to make sense of this whole thing, I stood there in disbelief. The thought of Bishop having his sister kidnapped just didn't sit right with me. He wasn't that type of person. He was down for his family, and from what I've seen, he loved them. Hell, the whole reason he came down to Virginia was to avenge his brother's death. That had to be some bullshit.

"Look, I don't know where you're getting your information from, but Bishop would never do anything to hurt his family, including his sister," I replied to Sean's accusations. "He's not that kind of guy. And now that I think about it, when he told me that Bria had gotten kidnapped a couple nights ago by some niggas that had a beef with him, he was really upset about it and I could tell by his actions that he was going to make them pay for it."

But Sean wasn't feeling my opinion or me. He made it painfully obvious that I needed to take a closer look at Bishop and his dealings. "Bishop is throwing the wool over your eyes," he stated. I could tell by the look in his eyes that he thought I was a fool or some lovesick bitch who didn't know head from tail. Evidently he didn't know I knew my way around the block.

"Well, since he's throwing the wool over my eyes, explain to me why he got mad when I told him that Bria might've tried to call me," I began. "Remember when we were eating last night and somebody called with a blocked number and I thought I heard a lady's voice tell me to help them?"

"I remember that all too well," he answered immediately. "But again, he's playing you like a deck of cards. He wants you to believe that he's upset and plans to settle the score with these imaginary thugs, so when the shit hits the fan he could use you as his alibi."

Still trying to wrap my mind around everything Sean was telling me, I began to feel sick.

My stomach was churning just thinking about the type of man I have gotten myself involved with this time. Will I ever find a guy who's not a killer and will love and respect me?

While I pondered on how my life had turned upside down, Sean unveiled the plan he had for me. "Lynise, we came at you today because we need you to help us find out where Bria is before something really bad happens to her," he said.

I placed my face in the palms of my hands. I figured if everything Sean was saying was true, then Bishop is more of a fucking psychopath than Duke. "I don't know, Sean," I said while I pondered the pros and cons of their mission for me. I figured if Bishop was involved with his sister's kidnapping, then getting rid of me wouldn't be hard at all. I wasn't his blood relative, nor was I his only girl. And needless to say, we didn't have kids together, and I didn't have anything to hold over his head. It would be really easy to put a bullet in my head, and Bishop wouldn't lose a wink of sleep over it. Being around him after finding out he was capable of causing his own sister's demise wasn't exactly what I wanted to put on my to-do list.

"What exactly do you need me to do?" I asked.

Agent Morris stepped forward. "All we need you to do is wear a wire and try to gather as much intel on the whereabouts of Bria and

Bishop's drug operation so we can bring the case to a close."

"What if he finds out that I'm helping y'all?" I asked.

"Don't worry too much about that. We have our surveillance set up inside of Sean's apartment and we'll be right there if anything goes wrong." Agent Morris tried assuring me.

"Can I speak to you in private for a second?" I asked Sean in front of the other agents.

"Yeah, sure," he replied, and then instructed the other agents to give us a minute to talk in private.

The agents got back inside of their black SUV. That gave me the green light to discuss my concerns with Sean in private. "What's really going on, Sean?"

"What do you mean?"

"Why didn't you tell me you were a federal agent in the beginning? Do you realize the position you put me in?" I expressed. I felt like a damn fool thinking he and I could've got together and started a fling. Stuff never works out the way we plan it.

Sean started shaking his head as if he was apologetic. "I know. Believe me, I wanted to tell you I was working undercover while we were eating breakfast yesterday. But I would've gotten my head ripped off by my supervisor if I had."

Frustrated by my situation, I turned around

to see if the other agents were still inside of the Suburban. They were. I also looked around the area. This was crazy. We were in plain sight at a gas station two miles from my apartment. I was sure somebody on the block would wonder what was up. I looked back at Sean and asked him if I really had to wear the wire, knowing how dangerous that could be for me. Bishop was no ordinary guy. I watched him murder my ex–best friend, Diamond, and slaughter Duke, so killing me would be next to nothing for him.

Sean looked like I was putting him under a lot of pressure to answer my question. But I wasn't going to let him get off that easy. I had to know if I had other options. "Sean, please don't make me wear that wire. I won't be able to act normal around Bishop with that thing taped to my body. Additionally, he and I are still romantic . . . sexual. So I know he'll start acting suspicious and find it."

I looked at him when I mentioned our sex life. He was a man, and I hoped Sean understood that men could be very spontaneous when it comes to sex.

"Lynise, I know who you are." He surprised me. "And I know about that case you were involved in back in Virginia. But I kept that a secret from everyone in my unit. I did that because we really need you to help us take Bishop down. After we are able to do that, then you're free to go on your way."

"What will happen if I don't?"

"I wouldn't be able to let you leave."

Stunned by Sean's response, I became bummed out that he'd hold this shit over my head. I mean, he basically told me if I didn't wear the fucking wire, then I'd be shipped back to Virginia. What kind of deal was that? He literally just shut me down. "You have got to be joking," I finally commented. "You are sending me on a suicide mission? He will chew me up and spit my ass out with no hesitation whatsoever."

"Agent Morris told you that we will be there in an instant if anything goes wrong."

I threw my hands in the air. "So that's it? Y'all will be there if something goes wrong. Do you know if he finds out I am wearing a wire, I'll be dead by the time you're able to kick in the fucking apartment door? He doesn't play around when he wants to get rid of some-one. He stops their life span in the blink of an eye," I warned Sean.

"Look, I understand how risky this could be, but if you remain calm and do what we tell you to do, then you'll be fine."

Realizing that I wasn't going to talk my way out of this fucking mission, I let out a long sigh and asked him when I was supposed to start wearing the wire.

"If you'll follow us to the federal building downtown, we'll set everything up. And then you can go on your way."

Sean waited for me to climb back into my car before he got into his SUV. And after he pulled out of the service station parking lot, I followed him while the other two federal agents followed me.

The police escort!

Chapter 9

What's Behind Door #1?

I thought I saw one of Bishop's partners following us down the road, but when I took a second look I realized it was some random guy going in the same direction as us. And when he passed us, I let out a sigh of relief.

Sean and the other two agents escorted me into an underground parking garage directly beneath the federal building. I climbed out of the car and took inventory of all the unmarked FBI vehicles parked in the garage. I had no idea the government had these agents driving such late model vehicles. I saw at least ten brand-new black Suburban trucks, six Dodge Chargers, and a couple of Tahoe trucks. There weren't any shabby vehicles in sight.

Now I realized where all the money seized by the government went.

"Lynise, we're gonna go through this door over here," Sean told me, pointing to a gray steel door.

I followed them through the door to an open floor of cubicles with wooden desks and modern office equipment. Sean led me to a conference room with a big screen mounted on the wall and a laptop computer placed on a table at the front of the room. I took a seat in the chair next to the table with the laptop and waited for Sean and the other agents to do their thing.

Of course Sean acted as if he ran things in the office. Before he allowed Agent Morris to place the wire device on me, he went into a spiel about how big it was, where they were hiding it, and how it worked. I was relieved when I saw that it was no bigger than a tube of ChapStick. It could be easily hidden and hard to detect on my body.

"Would you feel uncomfortable wearing it in the waist area of your pants?" Agent Morris asked me. "If you are, we can hide it in your hair."

"No way. That won't work. Put it around my waist," I instructed him.

I stood there and watched Agent Morris as he pinned the wiretap in the waistline of my pants. While he was steady at work, my Black-Berry rang. My heart skipped a beat. I knew without looking at the screen that the caller was Bishop. He was the only one with my number. Besides that, I knew he was probably calling me back about the phone call Keisha and I had earlier. Knowing him, he was going to apologize for her ill-mannered behavior and then he was going to ask me where I was. I knew him like a book—almost.

"Hello," I said.

"Where you at?" he didn't hesitate to ask.

"At the store," I lied. I tried to remain calm like nothing was going on. But Bishop wasn't stupid by a long shot. He sensed something wasn't right with me. So I quickly blamed it on my personal issues.

"Which one?" he continued.

"I'm at one of the local mom-and-pop shops right by the apartment. Why?"

"Because I wanted to come and hang out with you today."

I was shocked by his willingness to come and meet me so we could spend time together, and it made me feel uneasy. He never wanted to meet me in the streets. He always waited for me to get back to the apartment before we decided to do something together. While I talked to him, I motioned for the agent to hold off a minute from trying to secure the wiretap on me. I needed to concentrate and give Bishop my complete attention. Not only that, I didn't want him to hear any peculiar noises in the background.

"Oh really. Wow! This is a first. I don't know whether to smile or cry," I joked, hoping he'd stop probing me about my whereabouts.

"Look, I know I've been acting like an ass-hole lately, but I've been under a lot of stress since I got back home. So I wanna make it up to you by taking you out. Spend a little money on you and show you how much I appreciate you."

Taken aback by Bishop's sudden change in behavior, I put him on speaker to make sure I wasn't hearing things. I needed Sean and the other two agents to hear Bishop's exact words and tone to confirm that this whole thing was real. "Can you make sure your stalker girl-friend doesn't run up on us again?" I asked.

"Oh, yeah, about that," he began. "I really called you to apologize about the way she acted when you called earlier."

"I was pretty shocked that she answered your phone."

"Well, you don't have to worry about that anymore."

I chuckled a little to bring humor into the conversation. "You must've cursed her out like you did me."

He chuckled back at me. "Yeah, it was something like that."

"Okay, check it out. Let me pay for my things and I'll be back at the apartment before you know it."

"A'ight," he said, and then we both hung up.

Sean and the two other agents stood there and gave me a long, hard stare. Sean spoke up. "I hope you're not falling for that BS he just fed you."

"I don't think it was bullshit," I answered with confidence.

Sean shook his head while the other two agents smiled. "He's playing you big-time," he said.

"Y'all don't know him like you think you do. He's a good man and he has saved my life on more than one occasion."

"Sounds like she's having second thoughts," Agent Morris told Sean. The other agent remained quiet.

"Yeah, it definitely sounds that way, but she's aware that she has no other options," Sean replied to him.

"Well, let's get this show on the road," Agent Morris stated. Seconds later, he and the other agent resumed the task of planting the wire on me while Sean stood back and watched.

After the wire was secured around my waist, Sean gave me thorough instructions about how this device worked and how easy it was to remove and place in other clothing. "In the event he wants to have sex with you and wants to undress you, you are permitted to let him take off your shirt and your bra, but under no circumstances should you let him take off your pants. Try to distract him and do that part yourself, because if he brushes his hand on the device, he'll want to know what it is."

As I listened to these instructions, my armpits began to perspire heavily. It felt as if I was sitting in a fucking sauna. And the horrific images of him finding out what I was about to do gave me an instant headache. I even felt light-headed, so I sat in one of the office chairs and took a load off.

"Are you okay?" Sean asked me.

I started to tell him to go to hell, because in all honesty he didn't give a damn about whether I was okay or not. All he cared about was the fact that I was about to help him and his partners get more information on Bishop so they could arrest him on federal indictments. But I had a trick for their asses. I wasn't about to let Sean or those other two crackers use me and hold my Virginia situation over my head so they could make their case stick. No way. Fuck that.

"I'm fine. But I need to know how long y'all plan on me wearing this thing."

"Look at it this way," Sean began. "The sooner you get us what we're looking for, the sooner we can take it off."

Once I processed everything, I stood and asked if I could leave.

"Yes, you most certainly may," Sean replied. "But please keep in mind that we're not too far away from you if anything should go wrong.

And don't ever try to disconnect that wire, because if you do, we'll know it. And you will force us to blow your cover."

"Are you fucking kidding me? You mean to tell me that if I disconnect the wire, y'all are going to bum-rush my spot?"

"Most definitely. While you're under our surveillance, we abide by strict rules. It's important that we keep the line of communication open, so if it's compromised, then we have to react."

"What if I made a mistake and disconnected it?"

"It would be the same protocol."

"All of you motherfuckers with badges are the same," I told them, and then I grabbed my handbag from the chair. On my way out of the room, I rolled my eyes at everyone and then I walked out of there.

I'm a certified informant now! Ugh!

Chapter 10

Get Them Before
They Get You

I was shaking like a leaf dangling from a tree on a windy day. One part of me wanted to get on the nearest highway and drive in the opposite direction of the apartment. There was no way I'd be able to act normal around Bishop with this fucking wire strapped to my body like this, so what was I going to do? I had already been given a warning not to disconnect the wire, so that option went out of the window. Additionally, I wondered if this was how Bishop had found out about his sister being a snitch for the FBI.

Ten minutes into the drive Bishop called

me back, but when I said hello, he didn't respond. "Hello," I said once again, but he didn't respond.

I did hear a little bit of rumbling sounds in the background. Instead of saying hello, I yelled out his name, but he still didn't hear me. At that moment I realized his phone must've dialed my number by accident, so I disconnected the call.

Fifteen miles later, I arrived at the apartment, but Bishop's vehicle was nowhere in sight. I started to wonder why he called me and lied about being at the apartment when in fact he wasn't here. Was he playing some kind of game with me? Well, whatever it was, I wasn't amused by it at all.

Bishop's absence gave me some alone time to think about whether I would tell him about the feds and the wiretap. At the end of the day, it was either I let the feds take him down or I say to hell with being their confidential informant and allow them to send my ass back to Virginia. I knew if I did go back south, the homicide detectives could expose me, and that would be scary as well. They could very well be the corrupt cops that would sell me to the Carter brothers or the highest bidder. I swear that wouldn't be a good look at all for me. My life would definitely be nonexistent after that.

As I made my way down the sidewalk to the

apartment, I noticed through my peripheral vision a truck pulling into the parking lot. I tried to block the sudden pounding of my heart out of my mind, but my heart wouldn't allow it. I had to turn around to see who it was. When I looked over my shoulder and saw that it was Agent Sean Foster, I became irritated. My facial expression showed it. I gritted at the agent as hard as I could.

When I suddenly noticed Bishop had pulled up in the parking lot behind Sean, I damn near had a heart attack. I tried to straighten up my face immediately, but I knew it was too late. The look Bishop displayed gave me the impression that he had caught me in the act. When he looked over at Sean's truck, that gave me confirmation that I had indeed been caught.

How am I going to explain this? My mind raced.

I began to think of the many lies I could tell when Bishop popped the questions. I wasn't sure if I should go inside of the apartment or stay outside to greet him. In a matter of seconds, the thoughts were plentiful in my head. Then I just said *Fuck it.* I didn't want to bring on any extra drama, so I stood there and waited for him to approach me.

I tried my best to try to act like I was happy to see him. I even forced a smile. And when Sean finally got out of his truck to go inside his FBI-rented apartment, I didn't look his way.

Bishop, on the other hand, knew something wasn't right, and he made it his business to make mention of it. "What's up with you and that nigga?" he asked as he approached me.

By this time, Sean was inside of his place. But with the help of this wiretap attached to my clothing, I was sure he heard Bishop's question.

"What kind of question is that? I don't even know that man," I lied, hoping he'd second-guess his intuition and go with my word.

"Well, why the fuck you frown at that nigga when he pulled up?"

"I didn't frown at him," I continued. I tried to come across as sincere as I could.

I was nervous, but there was no way I was going to show it. The thing I learned about Bishop in Virginia is that the man has a sixth sense. There was a reason he was the kingpin in this area, and a bigger reason the Bureau was on his ass to arrest him. Once again, I thought about his sister. If he would off his own blood, I was an easier candidate to eliminate.

Bishop stood there and looked at me as if he could see right through me. But I stood my ground and played the role. There was no way

I was going to let him believe what he actually saw. No way!

"You sure you and that nigga ain't fucking around behind my back?" Bishop pressed the issue.

I laughed because Bishop was so fixated about whether Sean and I were seeing each other that he couldn't see the writing on the wall. And then I shook my head and mulled over the fact that if he only knew Sean was an FBI agent and he was Sean's main target, a war would've broke out.

"You are truly worried about the wrong thing," I commented, trying to deflect any indication that Sean and I had anything going on, much less knew each other. "Come on, let's go inside." I grabbed him by his hand and escorted him into the apartment.

Once we were inside, Bishop went directly to the bathroom and I went into the bedroom to calm my nerves. My mind was still a minefield of thoughts. Having a wiretap was nerve-racking as shit. I wondered if that was how Bishop found out about Bria—her mind was so fucked up about trying to get information from him and keep herself out of prison that she gave herself away. I said a quick prayer to God and asked Him to protect me while I was treading on these dangerous waters. I couldn't tell you whether He heard me, but after I said the words, Amen, I sure felt better.

After the toilet flushed, Bishop came out of the bathroom and went straight into the living room area, suspecting that's where I was. "Lynise, where you at?" he yelled.

I left the bedroom and met him in the hallway. "What's up?" I asked.

"You ready?" he asked.

"Yeah, I'm ready. But where are we going?" I wanted to know for my own peace of mind, as well as for Sean and his fellow agents. Plus, I didn't know the range of this ChapStick-size bug.

"I want you to make a run with me," he told me.

Curiosity piqued my interest, so I pressed the issue. "Make a run with you where?" I asked. I needed some answers. First, I knew it was my nerves goading him on. Second, a lot of stuff had happened in the last week and I was always getting limited information. I was tired of that shit. I wanted more concrete answers.

"I need you to make a pickup for me."

"What kind of pickup?" I probed.

Bishop gave me an odd look. "What's up with all the fucking questions? Whatcha an informant or something?" he asked.

After Bishop made the accusation about me being an informant, my entire body was consumed with fear. If I was ten years younger, there's no doubt I would've told on myself and showed him the wiretap. But since I had street sense and survival skills, I used reverse psychology on his ass and burst into laughter. "If I was an informant, I'd still be in Virginia working for those crackers instead of up here with your ass," I commented as I placed my right hand on my hip.

"Well, since you ain't no informant, then stop asking me questions," he replied, and then he walked to the front door and opened it. "Let's go."

I stared at the front door after Bishop walked outside and wondered what I had gotten myself into. Bishop had proven himself to be a violent man when necessary. He had also proven himself to be very loyal. So I couldn't imagine the wrath he'd cast down on me for being disloyal to him. It would be too damaging to my mental state to consider.

I grabbed my handbag and keys to the apartment and then I headed outside behind Bishop. He was standing by my car with his back facing me while he talked on the phone. I couldn't hear his conversation, so I tiptoed in his direction, hoping I could at least figure out at least who he was talking to. But by the time I got close enough to him to hear anything, he turned around and saw that I was coming and ended his call.

"I'ma call you back later after I take care of my business," I heard him say, and then he paused. "Yeah, I promise."

After he finished his call, I couldn't help but think that it wasn't business. I wasn't too happy about his private conversation, because I knew deep in my heart that he was talking to a chick. And from his facial expression, I knew it wasn't Keisha. He didn't smile all the time when he talked to her. Hell, I couldn't remember him smiling once in my presence when he talked to that bitch. That smile he wore had everything to do with a new chick. I would bet every dime I had that it was that bitch Chrissy.

As long as I've been old enough to fuck niggas, I've noticed that cats got real hyped and giddy when they got a new bitch in their lives. They called it *new pussy*, and every nationality of men went nuts over *new pussy*. But when the honeymoon phase was over, they started acting like damn fools and the *I love you*s stopped coming.

My heart wanted me to lash out at him, but I left well enough alone. I knew it would be an argument I wouldn't win anyway. "Are you driving?" I asked.

"Yeah, hand me the keys," he instructed.

I tossed the keys his way, and after he caught them he got inside the car and then he unlocked the passenger side door for me. Once he got on the road, he went south. I wasn't too familiar with the route he took, but I could read signs and I had a photographic memory, so if I had to come back this way, I'd remember.

Then I thought, maybe I wouldn't have to remember. Knowing I had been wired, I wondered if one of the agents besides Sean was following Bishop and me to God knows where. I still didn't know the distance my wiretap transmitted. I was sure there was no way they'd be able to listen in on the wiretap if I were miles and miles outside of their perimeter. My guess was that it was entirely impossible. But when it was said and done, I'd know for sure.

During most of the drive, our conversation was limited as we listened to Jay Z and Kanye West's CD. I did, however, get up the gumption to ask about Bria, since he hadn't brought her up since our last chat.

"Have you found out who has Bria?" I asked. It was important for me to know if he had made any attempt to find out who had his sister. I wasn't doing this to get information for the FBI. I did this for me. I needed to know if in fact he was behind her kidnapping.

It took him at least thirty seconds to answer my question, which, of course, didn't sit well with me. *Who hesitates to answer questions about a loved one in trouble?* I couldn't tell you why he did this. Was it to shield me from the gripping reality of what she was going through? Or because he was the one actually behind her getting snatched up? If so, was it because he found out she was working with the feds? But come rain or shine, the truth would come out. Or that was the lie old folks told us young folks.

"I don't want to talk about that right now," he finally said.

"Why not? She was kidnapped a few nights ago and you don't want to talk about it? That's crazy."

"What do you want me to say? We got her back and she's all right."

"That's exactly what I want to hear," I expressed.

"Well, I'm sorry, but I can't tell you that," he replied.

"So what are you going to do? Just leave her there? I mean, it's getting close to 72 hours, so somebody has to do something."

"Don't you think I know that?" Bishop snapped. "I loved my sister. She and I used to be really close growing up. She was closer to me than she was to Neeko. So don't ever question me about what I need to do concerning her. Leave that situation alone, unless I bring it up to you."

I sat there and listened to Bishop chastise me concerning his relationship with Bria. I became numb. I was thrown for a loop when he used certain words in past tense . . . *like she was gone.* I wanted to interject to get a better understanding about what he meant when he said *he loved her.* But I didn't for fear of his becoming suspicious of mc.

I wondered if Sean or the other agents had our conversation recorded. In my mind, Bishop had said some incriminating things. I guess I would find out sooner than later.

Am I my sister's keeper?

Chapter 11

The Replacement Courier

Bishop and I drove in silence after he put me on blast about Bria. I heard the rage in his voice when he instructed me not to ask him any more questions concerning her. For the first time, I feared him. I feared that whatever he did to her, he'd do to me without hesitation. Suspecting this, I knew I needed to regroup and come up with another plan. The plan the feds had strategized for me wasn't conducive for my well-being and I was going to take my life into my own hands.

To my surprise, Bishop pulled up behind a white, late model Jeep Cherokee parked in front of an old, gray townhouse in a run-down neighborhood on the north side of Newark. When I looked at the bumper and noticed the green bumper sticker, I realized the truck was a rented vehicle.

After Bishop put the car in park, he reached down in his front pants pockets and handed me a set of car keys. "I need you to get in that Jeep and follow me to my people's house, so we can drop it off," he instructed me.

"Okay," I said, and got out of his car.

As much as I didn't want to drive the truck, I was too nervous and too damn afraid to raise hell. Bishop watched me while I got into the truck and cranked the engine. Once he realized I had started the vehicle, he pulled out in front of me and led the way.

Before I pulled onto the road behind him, I looked over my shoulder to make sure there wasn't a car coming. That's when I realized that Sean was indeed on our tail. He was parked at least seven vehicles behind us. As soon as I pulled out onto the road, he made his way onto the road too. I was shaking my head at the stupidity. This motherfucker, Sean, should have realized that Bishop had seen him in the parking lot. Why take the chance and be spotted again? One of the other agents should have conducted the tail.

Then I found myself making excuses for Sean. Like Newark was damn near all-black and a white agent would stand out anywhere in this junky, smelly-ass city. With the exception of the business areas in Newark, the place was one big ghetto cesspool.

Since I was wired and I knew Sean could hear me, I wanted to mention that Bishop made the comment about *how he used to love his sister.* And how I was now on board with the FBI of suspecting Bishop as the cause of Bria's kidnapping. I had even wanted to say something about the possibility of her being dead. However, the feds already thought she was dead. And that thought brought my mind once again to the ChapStick-sized bug I had on my person. Was it the same kind that Bria had on when Bishop figured out she was a snitch? If so, why didn't Sean and his crew come to her rescue?

My mind being all over the place wasn't helping my nerves. I had to chill or possibly get myself killed. When I thought about how deep this situation was, I elected to keep my mouth closed. If Sean was close enough during our drive to pick up the truck, I was sure he heard my conversation with Bishop. All I wanted right now was to get out of this thing alive. I didn't think that was asking for too much.

While I followed Bishop I noticed there were at least fifteen Black Ice incenses dangling from the rearview mirror of the Jeep. There was no doubt he had them there to cover up the smell of what was obviously weed that he had in the truck. As a matter of fact, the scent was so strong, I had to roll down the window to get some ventilation. It seemed like the longer I was in this truck, the more alarmed

I got. I mean, there had to be at least ten pounds of weed in this vehicle. The thought of my being in possession of it made me a little upset. *Why the fuck couldn't he get Keisha's dumb ass to transport this shit? Am I more dispensable than her?* Okay, granted, I was a hood chick and I didn't have a lot to lose, but I was still somebody and he needed to recognize that.

Before we reached our location, Bishop called me on my cell phone and gave me final instructions. I pressed the speakerphone button so Sean could hear it as well.

"We're getting ready to pull up to a brown, brick two-story house on the right side, so I want you to pull up into the driveway and park the truck as close as you can to the back of the house. And when you're done, take the keys to the back door of the house and ask for a dude named Manuel. When he comes to the door, he's going to hand you a black bag, and after he does that, hand him the keys to the car and tell him that it's in the glove compartment and then you come back and get in my car."

"What do you want me to do if the guy Manuel isn't there?"

"Don't worry, he's there," Bishop assured me.

To confirm the instructions Bishop gave me, I repeated them back to him. "So all I have to do is drive the truck into the driveway and get as close to the back door as I can and then knock on the door and ask for Manuel?"

"Yup. But make sure he gives you the black bag before you hand him the keys to the truck."

"I got that part."

"Okay, well, do your thing so we can get the hell out of here."

"Roger that."

Even though the instructions Bishop gave me were quite simple, there was still a harsh reality that something could go wrong. Any time you were dealing with dope, whether it was marijuana, coke, or heroin, things didn't always go as planned. Look at how Bria got caught up in one of her deliveries. The feds jammed her up, made her turn against her brother, and now she's probably dead with her remains thrown in one of these neighborhood Dumpsters. What a terrible way to have your life come to a screeching halt.

In a matter of two and a half minutes, I had parked the rental truck at the end of the driveway and was at the back door knocking and waiting for this Manuel character to make the exchange.

When the door finally opened, a Puerto Rican–looking cat appeared before me. He was average height, around five eight or nine, sporting a white tee, a pair of blue denim jeans, and a pair of brown Timberland boots. While I was checking him out, he was checking me out as well.

"Are you Manuel?"

"That depends." He smiled. "Who are you?" He turned the question around on me.

"No disrespect, sweetie. But I was told to drop off that truck in your driveway and wait for Manuel to give me a black bag. Now, if you ain't Manuel, then will you tell him that someone is at the door waiting for him?"

He smiled. "Don't get bent out of shape, mommie! I'm Manuel," he said, and then he picked up a black bag from the floor behind the back door and handed it to me. "Here you go."

Once I had the bag in my hand, I handed him the keys to the rental truck. "This is for you. It's in the glove compartment," I said, ensuring I delivered the message Bishop wanted me to, and then I turned to leave.

"Hey, where is my girl, Bria? She's the one who normally run this route," he replied.

"I don't know," I told him, and kept walking toward the front of the house, where Bishop was parked.

Halfway to Bishop's car, I couldn't help but notice how heavy the black bag was. When I rubbed my hand across the side of it, I knew I was carrying a lot of cash. I couldn't tell you how much it was, but it was a lot. And that's all I needed to know.

As soon as I got back into the car with Bishop, he immediately grabbed the bag from me and stuffed it underneath the driver seat, and then he drove off.

I was so excited about the money, I didn't check to see if Sean was parked down the street watching me walk back to the car. My mind was on money. The entire trip back I was thinking about getting my hands on some of the cash in that bag. I didn't know what kind of deal he had with Bria. But I did know she didn't want for anything and she always talked about having her own money. I knew she wasn't making bank as a beautician, so this was her second job, per se.

Getting a piece of the prize was suddenly on my mind, so much so I didn't even check to see if Sean was behind us or anywhere in the vicinity when we made it back to the apartment.

Had I fucked up getting in bed with the feds versus getting paid?

Back at the apartment, Bishop went into the bedroom and closed the door. He stayed in there for about fifteen minutes and then he returned to the living room, where I was watching television. He had the black bag folded underneath his left armpit.

"I'll be back in thirty minutes, so be ready to go when I get back."

"All right," I said with little enthusiasm.

To be frank about the situation, I was kind of glad he left me in the apartment. The way I was beginning to see him was an ugly sight. The thought of him using me to do his dirty work and take the place of Bria was mind-blowing.

Manuel definitely confirmed my worst fear. To know that he was unaware of her kidnapping sent chills through my entire body. *Why hadn't Bishop told Manuel about Bria's abduction? Did he have something to hide?* I swear this picture Bishop was painting of himself was getting uglier by the moment.

While I sat there and tried to piece together this puzzle, there was a knock on the door.

Startled by the knocking, I got up from the sofa and answered the door. I wasn't surprised to see Sean. But I was shocked that he would take the chance to come here when Bishop hadn't been gone that long.

Paranoia and fear consumed me. "What are you trying to do, get me killed?" I snapped.

"Of course not. I wouldn't let that happen."

"Do you realize Bishop just left not too long ago?"

"Look, don't worry about that. I've got two female agents a couple of blocks from here monitoring who comes in and goes out of this place. And from what they told me, he's heading north on Mount Prospect Avenue."

Overwhelmed by everything that was going on around me, I sighed at Sean and said, "Well, what do you want from me now?"

"I came here to make sure that you are okay."

"Do I look like I'm okay? I mean, I am walking around with a wire stuck to my clothing. Which, of course, has put my life in danger."

"Lynise, please calm down. You will be fine. We are less than one hundred feet away from you. So there is no way we will let any harm come upon you."

"I'm sure you said those same words to Bria," I replied sarcastically.

"Look, let's stay focused. Because what I am about to ask you is very critical."

I sucked my teeth. "What is it?" I asked, not really wanting to hear his reply.

"Do you know if you were transporting drugs to that drop-off location you just left?"

"I'm sure I was."

"What makes you so sure?"

"Because he had over a dozen Black Ice incenses dangling from the rearview mirror so he could cover up the smell."

"Could you tell what it was?"

"No, I couldn't," I lied. "The incense smell was too strong. They almost gave me a fucking headache, which is why I rolled down the driver's side window."

"I heard him tell you to tell the guy Manuel that the stuff was in the glove compartment. But did he indicate how much was in there?"

"No. I was only told to relay the message, ask for the black bag, and then hand the guy the keys to the rental."

"Did you know what was in the black bag?"

"It felt like a lot of money."

"Could you tell about how much it was?"

"No."

"Well, while you were at the back door, were you able to see into the house?"

"Yes, a little bit. Why?"

"Could you see how many people were in there?"

"I only saw one other guy besides Manuel. But I heard that guy talking to someone else."

"So you're saying that there were two other guys in the house with Manuel."

"Yeah. That's exactly what I'm saying."

"Okay. I think that's all I need."

"So I get to take this wire off?"

"No, of course not. We're not done yet."

"But you just said that's all you needed."

Sean chuckled at me, amused by my comment. "I wasn't talking about the case itself. I was talking about the drop-off you just made."

"So what happens now?"

"You gotta get more information for us."

"Haven't I gotten enough? I practically got Bishop to admit that Bria was dead. And that he had something to do with it."

"No. He didn't admit to anything. Telling you he loved her and that they were really close will not tell the judge or jury that he murdered her. Now it tells us that he had something to do with her disappearance. But we need more than that. We need something concrete, like her body with his DNA all over it or a confession. If we can't get that, then we are fighting an uphill battle."

I stood there with the most disgusted expression I could muster up. I had no words for Sean. So the only thing that was left for me to do was to shake my head at him.

Noticing how upset I had become, he ended our little chat by saying, "It will all be over soon. Oh, and by the way, even though you couldn't get a confession, I commend you for getting him to give us an idea about whether she was still alive."

"Oh really! Is that it?" I replied sarcastically.

He smiled. "What else do you want? I've already given you a get-out-of-jail-free card. Be happy with that."

I was burning up inside thinking about how the niggas with badges were more crooked than the niggas in the streets. Sean had just confirmed how they couldn't care less about the well-being of their informants. All they cared about was using them to make their cases and then they throw them to the fucking wolves.

I was sure he treated Bria the same way. And by that, I knew she was made to turn on her brother for those bastards. But guess what? Fuck them and their motherfucking case, because I was going to have the last fucking laugh.

As far as Bishop was concerned, I realized he was about Bishop. He didn't give a fuck about me or the next bitch. And when it was all said and done, he'd figure out that I didn't give a fuck about him too. It was all about Lynise from this day forward.

I'm not to be trusted!

Chapter 12

I Didn't See This Coming

Bishop returned an hour and a half later. I had taken a shower and changed into a pair of white jeans and a very colorful V-neck T-shirt. Normally, I would wear a pair of classy sandals with three- to four-inch heels. But after all the drama I had attracted from Bishop's other woman, Keisha, and the feds, I decided to wear Nike running sneakers, just in case I had to fight or make a run for it. Before I left the apartment, I made sure the wire was secure around the waistband of my jean shorts. I wasn't about to have any mix-ups . . . because my life depended on it.

It was Thursday morning and Bishop's idea to drive into New York. I was really shocked when he jumped on the New Jersey Turnpike and headed north. One half of me was excited, but the other half became a little paranoid. I figured anything could happen to me in New York and there was nothing the feds could do to stop it. *Was he taking me there to test my loyalty to him once again? Or did he just plan to take a load off and show me a good time?* I didn't have the slightest clue, so I hoped and prayed that Sean or the other agents weren't too far behind us.

Shortly after we arrived in New York, Bishop suggested we go to his favorite Japanese restaurant, Benihana. Japanese food was one of my favorites, so I welcomed the idea.

When we pulled up to the restaurant in downtown Manhattan, he handed one of the valet drivers his keys to the car and then we went inside. Everything from the food to the service was excellent. I hadn't had this much fun in a very long time. Immediately after we left the restaurant, Bishop took me on a tour of Manhattan and then we ended up driving to Harlem.

"I need to make a quick stop and then we'll head back to Newark," he told me.

My mind quickly went into overdrive when he told me he needed to make a quick stop. I wasn't stupid. I knew that meant he needed to make either a drug pickup or contact with his drug connection. I had been with enough drug dealers to know that no one made deals over the phone. Deals were made in person. So that's exactly what Bishop wanted to do.

I thought we would be going to one of the projects in the city, but I was wrong. Bishop had to meet his connection at this Cuban restaurant in Spanish Harlem. There were at least ten Hispanic men standing outside the restaurant. I could tell that some of them were runners and the other ones were the lookout. Some of them looked to be sixteen, while the others appeared to be eighteen or older. After Bishop exited the car, one of the guys escorted him into the restaurant. I sat there and watched as the operation unfolded.

My heart began to race while I sat in the running car all alone. Between watching the guys standing outside the restaurant and watching the prostitutes working their magic on the opposite corner, I wondered whether Sean and the other agents followed us to the city, and whether they had this place under surveillance as well.

The traffic going in and out of area was an easy target for the feds. I would hate to be in the area when the agents tried to shut it down. I could see these young guys pulling out all the stops to keep themselves from going down, which, at worse, would start a vicious war.

I twiddled my thumbs for a full twenty minutes while I waited for Bishop's return. And just when I was about to go inside the restaurant to see why it was taking him so long, he came walking back outside with a brown paper bag in hand, looking like he had just ordered a meal to go. He was smiling from ear to ear. If I hadn't known better, I would've thought that he'd just won the fucking lottery.

"What are you so happy about?" I asked the moment he got back into the car.

"I'm happy because today has been a prosperous day for me," he replied, and then he sat the brown paper bag on the floor in the back. He put the control stick in drive and then pulled onto the road. "Ready to go back to Jersey?" he continued as he maneuvered in and out of traffic.

"I was ready to go back to Jersey after we ate at the restaurant," I expressed.

"Well, don't worry. I'll have you back at the crib in no time."

"I take it that you're going to drop me off."

"Yeah. But it's only for a little while. And after I make a few runs, then I'll come back to spend some time with you."

He reached over and rubbed my left side. As he worked his way up my thigh I knew he would try to stick his hand down the front of my shorts so he could feel on my pussy and get it wet. But I grabbed his hand and stopped him before things got out of hand.

"No, don't do that. You know you're gonna get my panties soaking wet," I whined, trying to play hard to get.

"That's what I want you to do," he replied as he continued to rub his hand on my thigh.

"Don't start something you can't finish," I threatened jokingly. The wire was hidden right below the button of my shorts. If Bishop would've gotten wind of that, I'd be for certain a dead bitch. God knows there's nothing I'd be able to do to stop him from killing me.

During most of the drive back to Jersey, I had to wrestle Bishop's hands from touching me in the wrong places. Luckily, his cell phone rang. It was like music to my ears. From the moment he answered, I knew it was a business call. He tried to speak in codes, but being a chick from the streets I was able to read between the lines. I was sure if Sean or the other agents were listening, then they knew what time it was too, assuming they could speak *street*.

"You will not believe what I got my hands on," he said to the caller. "It's ripe and ready to go."

I couldn't hear anything the caller was saying in return, but I heard him laughing, so I figured he was happy with the news Bishop had just given him.

Before Bishop hung up the phone, he instructed the caller to call all of his people and tell them to get ready because they were about to get some money.

After Bishop got the caller pumped up, I heard him shouting on the other end with pure excitement. For a minute there, I wanted to get excited for them. But when I looked casually through the passenger side mirror and noticed the two white FBI agents following us down the New Jersey Turnpike, I lost all enthusiasm. They reminded me that there wasn't a thing about my situation to be excited about. Just that thought snapped me back to reality.

To my surprise, that reality wasn't as jaw dropping as the one I was about to get. Not long after Bishop hung up, he started acting really weird. When he pressed down on the accelerator and began to look at his rearview mirror every other second, I knew he suspected that we were being followed.

I tried to act as normal as I possibly could, but his actions made me uncomfortable. I couldn't pretend that I hadn't noticed how he was acting.

"What's wrong with you?" I asked. I said it in a tone that made him realize that I was really concerned.

"I'm cool," he said. But his body language said something different.

"Well, if you're cool, then what are you trying to see in your rearview mirror? You've looked at it at least a dozen times since you got off the phone."

"I'm trying to see if those two crackers in that black Suburban are following me."

"Where are they?" I said, and then I turned to my left to look over my shoulder. But midway through my turn, Bishop stopped me.

"Don't look back! They might see you!" he shouted.

"I wasn't going to turn all the way around," I assured him.

"Look, don't draw any attention to us. If you wanna see who I'm talking about, then look in your side mirror. They're four cars behind us."

I leaned forward just a little bit and acted as if I was trying to get a glimpse of the two white men Bishop had become leery of.

"Can you see them?" he asked.

"Yeah. I see them. But why would they be following us?" I asked, trying to play the dumb role. I did this to see if he would come clean with the real reason why we went to New York. But he didn't fall for my tactic.

"I don't know," he answered as he continued to look over his shoulder and at the rearview mirror.

I could count the number of times using all of my fingers and toes that he looked back at the feds while they followed us. I tried to make him relax a little, but my attempts fell short. Thank God they decided to make a detour after tailing us for over twenty-five minutes. I believe if they would've stayed with us for at least ten more minutes, Bishop would have caused a major accident on this very busy highway, leaving a lot of innocent people hurt, or worse, dead.

I let out a sigh of relief after they were gone. Although I knew I'd see them in the near future, the thought of getting back to the apartment in one piece was good enough for me.

Thank God for blessings!

Chapter 13

Back at the Crib

Inoticed Sean's vehicle wasn't parked in its designated spot when Bishop and I arrived back at the apartment. I couldn't help but wonder where he was and what he was up to. He was the head investigative agent assigned to Bishop and his crew. Was he also following us? Sometimes the cops and feds used multiple cars when tailing a suspect. So I figured wherever he was and whatever he was doing was probably an effort to wrap this case up.

In the apartment, Bishop sat the bag down on the kitchen table and then went into the bathroom. Immediately after I heard his piss hitting the toilet water, I quickly turned my attention to the bag. The wheels in my mind were spinning like crazy. Curiosity was eating away at me like an energized Ms. Pac-Man ate her enemies. I wanted to look inside that bag so bad. The only thing that stopped me from doing so was the fact that Bishop had bionic ears and he would hear the bag rattle as soon as I touched it.

So once again I found myself leaving well enough alone. Hell, I already knew there were drugs inside of it. I couldn't tell you which kind, but I knew there was a lot of it. Whoever Bishop was talking to while we were on our way back from New York had already been forewarned that they were about to get paid.

Bishop's cell phone started ringing the exact same time he was coming out of the bathroom. "What's good?" he asked the caller.

I was sitting on the living room sofa. When he came into the living room, his whole mood changed. I couldn't hear what the caller was saying to him, but I could tell that Bishop was spooked. He stood in the middle of the floor and looked at me as if he could see directly through me. My heart rate picked up instantly, and I could feel my entire body began to perspire.

I wanted to ask him what was wrong, but my lips wouldn't move. Then I thought about how I was going to get out of that apartment alive if that call pertained to me.

I knew I wouldn't be able to get away from him on foot, because he could run faster than me. But maybe if I was able to knock him out with something that would put him out of commission for at least a couple of minutes, if not longer, I'd be able to do a homestretch.

While my mind was going haywire and I was contemplating my escape, Bishop finally opened his mouth and said, "I can't believe that that shit just happened. Me and Lynise just left that spot a few hours ago. And you mean to tell me that them crackers ran up in there that quick? Yo, I swear, somebody around us is either talking their asses off or those crackers were onto them long before we started throwing business their way."

After Bishop gave his spiel, he fell silent and listened to the caller. Once again, I couldn't hear what the caller was saying. When Bishop turned away from me and walked back into the kitchen, he made it almost impossible for me to get the scope of things surrounding the conversation.

The upside to this whole situation was that I had no prior knowledge about that drop-off I made to that guy, Manuel, until we were in route to his spot. If Bishop wanted to point fingers and find someone to blame, then it wouldn't be me.

What a joy that was to me. That thought was like music to my ears. Now I could exhale and relax, knowing that I was okay for the moment.

During his conversation, Bishop made it crystal clear how angry he was, and then he swore he would find out who was behind Manuel's spot getting ransacked by the police.

"Man, I swear to God, I am going to find out who snitched them niggas out like that," Bishop began. "Because that shit looks really bad on my part. It wouldn't shock me if them niggas think I did. And I can't have that shit over my head. Niggas around here would lose respect for me if they thought I had something to do with them niggas getting arrested. And check it, we can't blame this shit on baby girl, because she's out of the picture. So whoever did this knew about the drop right after Manuel gave us the green light."

After listening to the caller, Bishop said, "I understand all of that, but we have nothing to worry about. Even though the truck is in her name, they can't link it back to us, because she's not here. Now take a load off and fire up one of those expensive-ass cigars you got and call it a night. Oh yeah, don't forget to change your number. The way Manuel's spot got shut down, we could never be too careful. Who knows, the feds could put so much pressure on that nigga that he'll bitch up and rat all our asses out. And with everything we got going on, we can't have that."

The caller finished off his conversation with a few more words, and after Bishop told him that he planned to change his cell phone number as well, they ended their call.

Immediately after Bishop pressed the end button, he grabbed the bag from the kitchen table and walked back into the living room, where I was pretending to watch TV. He knew I heard bits and pieces of his conversation, so he stopped in the middle of the floor with a blank look on his face and asked me if I remembered leaving anything inside of that Jeep Cherokee truck before I got out of it.

I thought for a second before I answered him. And when I realized that I hadn't, I told him no.

"Are you sure?" He pressed the issue.

"Yeah. I'm positive. Why?"

Bishop hesitated for a moment as if he wasn't sure he wanted to tell me what was going on. So I gave him this look of reassurance, as if to say that whatever he told me would not leave the room and that I had his back when he needed it most.

"I just found out from my homeboy that the feds ran up in Manuel's spot about an hour after we left."

"Really?" I replied.

"Yeah. And I just heard they had the rental truck towed away."

"Oh, my God! Is that why you asked me if I had left something in the truck?"

"Yeah. I would hate for you to get pulled

into some shit you ain't got nothing to do with. The police up north are different from the police down south. If they had the slightest idea that a nigga is making some serious money, they will run up on you like they're about to rob you and split your motherfucking head right open in the process."

"They are all the same to me," I commented.

Bishop tucked the folded bag underneath his armpit and said, "Not to me. The fucking crackers up here are so grimy that they go after family members and turn everyone against each other to create division. And then the next thing you know, you're left with the choice to either kill your loved one or let them live. And I don't like that shit! I was raised on the principles that family is all you got. And when that's gone, you ain't got nothing else. So, it's downhill from there."

Chills ran through my body after Bishop's indirect confession about Bria. But what was even more chilling was the fact that he didn't blink when he opened up about his family. I could say that I saw a genuine spark in his eyes that declared his feelings concerning his family versus his freedom on the streets.

"And do you wanna know what's really crazy?" he asked.

"What?"

"Remember when I noticed that those two crackers were following us from New York?"

"Yeah."

"Yo, I will bet you every dollar I got in my pocket that those motherfuckers was following us because of that bust they had at Manuel's spot. I mean, it couldn't be a coincidence that Manuel's spot got shut down and then a few hours later we're being followed. Shit just doesn't happen like that, Lynise."

"Well, in my experience, I've never seen the police follow somebody and then leave them alone and then go into another direction. Usually if they follow you it means they want to make you nervous enough to commit a traffic violation to give them grounds to stop you. And then from there they got probable cause to do what the hell they want. And those white guys you said was following us didn't do any of that. So I think you're reading too much into that whole Turnpike situation."

"Look, I'm not saying you ain't right, but something on the inside of me is saying that the heat is on. So I'm gonna have to be extra careful, because it could've been anybody that set Manuel up. And I swear on everything I love that if I find out who it is, they're gonna end up in a cold and dark place. And they will never see the light of day again."

Oh, my God. The wish for death I saw in Bishop's eyes was extremely scary. And not only that, I couldn't believe how fast Bishop was starting to put two and two together. I knew he was quick on his feet, but I had no idea he would associate one thing with the other. I just hoped that since our conversation was being recorded by Sean and his other agents, maybe they would step back a little bit before this whole thing blew up in all of our faces prematurely.

As I watched Bishop, I felt as if I were living in the Twilight Zone. "I'm going to need you to hold the fort down until I come back," he told me.

"How long are you going to be gone?"

"I can't say right now. I've got too much shit on my mind and too much shit to do with little time to do it. So I'll call you once I get a minute."

"All right," I said to him, and then he left.

The day had been one fucking roller coaster ride for me. And to know that because of my wiretap, niggas were getting locked up left and right. Shit! Who knew Sean would go out and secure arrest warrants and bag up Manuel and his boys? I mean, I kind of knew, but I didn't know for sure, if that makes any sense.

I had heard that the difference between the feds and local cops was the feds moved faster. They would sit back and make the case like cops, but when it was time to make a move, they did exactly that—they made a move with arrests and warrants and everything else.

I was officially a *snitch* now.

Regarding how far this whole thing was going to go, I really couldn't say. I never signed up to get another cat and his boys locked up, but of course Sean had his own way of doing things, and he had made it painfully clear that I had no say whatsoever.

It would satisfy my curiosity if I knew how Sean and the other agents planned to take down Bishop and his crew. I also wanted to know where in the hell Bria was. In so many ways, Bishop had made references that she was gone. Any subject pertaining to her was always stated in the past tense.

I hoped and prayed that her body wouldn't turn up in the back of an alley somewhere. That would have really devastated the hell out of me.

Another thing that would have devastated me was if Sean used me to work his case and still turned me over to Detectives Morris and Paxton. Those doughnut-eating sons-of-bitches weren't worth shit! They didn't care about anyone unless they were feeding their dumb asses with tons of information so they could make their arrests. And the same could be said about the feds around here. I wished I could pile all of them up in a boat and set all of their asses on fire and let them burn to death. That would be the best thing ever. But I had to chill and be on my best behavior.

As the day wound down, I became a little more relaxed. In doing so, I decided to take off the wire. I didn't disconnect it, but I removed it from my clothes and hid it underneath

my dirty clothes in the bathroom hamper.
Bishop never went through my things. So I had
no worries. From there, I lounged around in
the apartment and tried to figure out my next
move.

Working on Plan A!

Chapter 14

Making Moves

Several hours passed and there was no word from Bishop. I was the type of chick that wanted to know a person's every move. It bothered the hell out of me that I was sitting in limbo wondering what was going on outside that front door. The only information I had to go on was that Sean and the other agents had rushed into Manuel's spot and shut it down. Other than that, I was in the blind.

While I lay across the sofa, my mind wandered off and I started thinking about my ex–best friend, Diamond, and how close she and I used to be. I wasn't feeling any remorse about her death, but I wondered why she allowed that nigga, Duke, to come between us. He wasn't worth shit! But he still managed to interfere with what she and I had. Too bad we couldn't turn back the hands of time, because not everything Diamond and I went through was bad. We actually had some damn good times together. But that's just it. Memories.

In addition to my memories of Diamond, I couldn't help but wonder what was going on back in Virginia. I didn't have anyone I called a friend. Plus, I didn't have a relationship with any of my family members. So, basically, I couldn't pick up the phone and call anyone back in Virginia and see what was up.

Then it dawned on me to call Lil Rodney. I knew he'd have an earful to tell me if I was able to get him on the phone. It wouldn't be unusual for his cell phone number to be disconnected or out of service. It was normal for cats who hustled in the streets to change their cell phone number every other month. This method kept the cops from wiretaps and unsolicited drug buys from informants. After I dug his number out of my handbag, I dialed it without blocking my cell phone number. It wouldn't have done me any good to block my number, especially if I found out that his cell phone number still worked. Blocking it would've been a sure way for him to send me straight to voice mail.

I was surprised to hear him answer on the second ring. "Yo, who dis?" he asked.

"Hey, Rodney, it's Lynise. What's up?" I replied with excitement. It felt good to hear a familiar voice.

"Who?" he inquired. He made it obvious that he didn't remember who I was or recognize my voice.

"Lynise. Remember? I'm Diamond's old roommate."

"Oh, yeah, what's good, shorty?"

"Nothing much. I'm chilling. What's going on in your neck of the woods?" I asked him.

"Yo, shit has been crazy around here. Right after that shit happened in your old spot, it's been hot as fire. The police been picking up niggas left and right out here. They figured since ain't nobody giving them the names of the people who ran up in that spot and put that slug in your homegirl's head, they gon' be assholes and harass everybody they see on the block."

"I am so sorry everybody is going through that dumb shit!"

"Come on now, you know we soldiers out here. We ain't about to let them fools run us off our block. Hell, naw! That shit ain't gon' happen."

"Anything else going on? Like, has my name been ringing in the streets?"

"I haven't heard it in a while. But right after that shit went down, a couple of the bitches that live out here started running their fucking mouths."

"What were they saying?"

"They started talking about how you set Diamond up and that her family is looking for you. Then I heard a couple of niggas at the dice game last week talking about how some cats named AC and TC were looking for you too because you fucked up their money."

"Who were the niggas that said that bullshit? Because they don't know what the hell they're talking about. First of all, I haven't fucked up nobody's money. And the second thing is, I don't even know who the hell AC or TC is. So tell those niggas to get their facts straight!" I snapped.

It was upsetting to know that rumors were being spread around about me and I wasn't there to confront them head on. Although I had just lied about not knowing who AC and TC were, I hadn't had any one-on-one contact with those guys, much less screwed up their money. So whoever was stirring up that bullshit needed to stop now.

"AC and TC are those two brothers that got the whole Norfolk on lock. They own a couple of businesses, but they get most of their money on the streets. And that nigga, Duke, was working for them too."

"Oh really?" I said, even though I knew the inside scoop on that situation.

"Yeah, that's what I heard. And I heard that he was supposed to make a half-a-million dollar run to them cats the night he got killed. So they are mad about that shit! I heard they're making a lot of niggas pay for it."

"That's messed up."

"I know."

"Did any of her family come by there to get her stuff out of the house?"

"Yeah, I saw a couple of older ladies go in there, but they only walked out of there with her clothes, because a couple of dope fiends from the other side of the park went in the day after the coroner took her body out and stole a lot of shit like two flat-screen TVs, a laptop, a Blu-ray player, her cable box, and a toaster oven."

"Get the fuck out of here. Who takes a cable box and a toaster oven?"

"Dope fiends."

"That shit is crazy!" I replied as I visualized the drug addicts ransacking my old apartment with Diamond's blood splattered all over the floors just to find every valuable thing they could sell to get their next fix. That was some bold shit to do.

"Yo, shorty, I gotta get off this phone. Got some people coming my way to score."

"All right. Handle your business. But this is my number that came through on your phone, so call me if you hear my name ringing on the streets again."

"A'ight. I gotcha," he assured me, and then we both disconnected the call.

I sat back and thought about our entire

conversation and came to the conclusion that I could never go back to Virginia. Not only were the police looking for me, but so was AC and TC. They were literally accusing me of making them lose their money because I was the motivating factor in Duke getting killed. Were they fucking insane? Duke was killed because of his involvement with Neeko and Katrina's deaths. So why use me as a pawn in their blame game?

Thank God I had Rodney's cell phone number. He was definitely a trooper and a lifesaver. Without him, I would have gotten railroaded a long time ago. I just hoped he'd keep his nose clean in the streets, because niggas don't play fair. So it would be a travesty if he became a fallen soldier. That would fuck my head up for sure.

Approximately forty-five minutes after I hung up my call with Rodney, I got another unexpected knock on the front door. I knew it was Sean, so I got up from the sofa and opened the door without peeking through the peephole. Just like I figured, Sean was the person behind the knock.

He smiled at me, so I asked him what he wanted from me now.

He answered, "What's up? How come we're not able to hear what's going on in this apartment?"

"Because I took the wire off my clothes."

"Where is it?" he asked, and then he stormed by me and entered the apartment.

I turned around and watched him as he stood in the middle of the living room floor. "It's in the bathroom tucked away in the dirty clothes hamper."

"Why is it in there?" he roared.

"Because I had to take a shower. And I just forgot to put it back on since Bishop wasn't here," I lied. I could tell he sensed that I was lying too.

"That's bullshit and you know it!" he snapped. "Do you know that you are tampering with government evidence? And that you could get some serious time for that?"

"First of all, who the hell do you think you're talking to like that? When I was pressured to wear that fucking wiretap you never said that I would have to go through this verbal abuse. And then on top of that, you're acting like I disconnected the damn thing."

"It does not matter if you disconnected it or not. Any time you take it off to take a shower or to change clothes, it is imperative that you put it back on. We cannot risk you leaving it hanging around and Bishop finding it."

"He wouldn't go looking in a dirty clothes hamper for anything."

"There's a first time for everything. Now go in there and get it. And when I put that wire back on you, you better not take it off until you and Bishop are seconds away from fucking each other's brains out. "

Inside I laughed at Sean's thunderous display. But I wasn't the least bit intimidated by his tone, nor was I afraid of him. However, when an unexpected voice tore through the atmosphere, I damn near wanted to faint.

"Lynise, who the fuck is this? And why he about to put a wire on you?" I heard the voice say.

It seemed so unreal. And I instantly closed my eyes and thought of a prayer, asking God to please let this be a dream. But when I opened my eyes back up and looked into Sean's face, I knew the voice I had just heard was, in fact, real . . . very real.

In slow motion, I witnessed Sean as he pulled his gun from the holster inside of his jacket, which in turn led me to believe that we were in deep trouble and shit was about to hit the fan. My heart sunk into the pit of my stomach when I saw Bishop's right-hand man, Torch, through my peripheral vision.

When I saw Torch pull his gun from his waist, I tried to take off in Sean's direction, but before I could move one inch, I was snatched backward and lost my balance in the process. Torch grabbed me around my neck with his left arm while he buried the barrel of his gun in the back of my head.

Here I was standing in between two men with guns drawn. Before I knew it, my life had flashed before my very eyes. "Put your gun down and let her go now, before I shoot," Sean threatened.

"Fuck that! You put your motherfucking gun down!" Torch demanded.

"Torch, please let me go," I whispered, my voice barely audible. I was shaking. The pain behind the force that Torch used to put the gun barrel at my head was beyond excruciating.

"Naw, motherfucker! You put your gun down!" Torch roared back at Sean. I couldn't believe I was in the middle of a fucking standoff. Who would've thought that I'd be between two niggas with guns? Not to mention that I'd be one bullet away from meeting my maker.

"Torch, please let me go," I managed to say again over all the yelling back and forth.

"Shut the fuck up, bitch!" Torch growled as he pushed the gun farther into my head. Spit was shooting from his mouth with every word he uttered.

I couldn't believe this shit was happening. I don't know how long it was—maybe a minute or two, which seemed like forever—before Torch realized Sean wasn't putting his gun down. So he began to step backward out the front door, dragging me along with him. I realized he was about to make a run for it and bring me along as his hostage, and I knew that would be terrible. Torch taking me away and hand-delivering me to Bishop, exposing me as the snitch, would end in a bloody murder—and I would be the victim.

I couldn't let that happen, so while he dragged me across the door seal, I grabbed the doorknob and held on for dear life. Of course that didn't work. Torch was much stronger than I was. With one pull from him, I had to let the doorknob go. From there, I saw my life slipping away.

"Help me!" I cried out to Sean. I knew what Torch was capable of. And it was nothing good. I'd witnessed him, along with Bishop and Monty, kill those people back in Virginia. So I refused to be his next victim.

Thank God, Sean felt my sentiments. Because immediately after Torch dragged me outside of the apartment, he was stopped in his tracks. "Put the gun down before we blow your fucking head off!" I heard a man's voice yell.

I couldn't see what was going on behind me, but when I felt Torch taking the gun from my head, I knew everything was about to be all right.

"Get the gun from him," Sean instructed.

After Torch had been disarmed and handcuffed, the two FBI agents identified themselves, notified him he was under arrest, escorted him back into the apartment, and sat him down on the living room sofa.

I tried to avoid eye contact with Torch. No one liked a snitch. But that didn't stop him from staring me down. I sat in one of the chairs in the kitchen, but I was still within sight of Torch. As I sat there, I witnessed him gritting at me through my peripheral vision. His facial expression spoke volumes to me. I could tell he had hatred toward me. I could only imagine what he was saying in his mind.

Meanwhile, Sean and one of the white agents excused themselves into the bathroom, so they could talk in private, while the other agent stood guard over Torch.

"All I need to know is how in the hell did he get past everyone on the surveillance team?" I heard Sean ask Agent Morris.

"I can't answer that. But I'll find out," Morris replied.

"Yes, please do, because we could've had a fatality tonight. And our whole investigation would've gone up in smoke," Sean continued.

During the next several minutes, I heard them talk over a couple other issues about how they had to get Torch out of the apartment before Bishop decided to come back. They also discussed what charges they were going to impose on Torch and how they planned to keep him from contacting Bishop or anyone else in his crew if he decided not to cooperate with their investigation. While Sean and Morris tried to line things up, Torch had a few words he had to say as well.

"Bitch, you ain't gotta look at me, but I see you!" he yelled. "And as soon as Bishop finds out about your snitching ass, you're gonna wish that you were dead!"

Even though I heard him, I did my best to ignore him by looking in the opposite direction. The agent standing guard over him tried to intercept Torch's loud outburst. "Shut the fuck up before I shove this gun down your throat," he threatened.

"You think I'm scared of your fucking gun? Do it! I dare you, you fucking punk!" Torch snapped.

Sean and Morris rushed out of the bathroom when they heard the commotion between Torch and the other agent. "I see you got your buddies running here to help you," Torch continued.

I wanted to get away from all the chaos, so I got up from my chair and went into my bedroom. But that didn't stop Torch from hurling derogatory comments at me. "Bitch, you can run and hide, but I can smell a rat anywhere."

The tone of his voice made it painfully clear that he would eat me alive if given the chance. For the first time in my life, I could honestly say I was glad the feds were here to intervene. Sean and the other agents saved my life. Then again, I thought, if Sean hadn't come to the door, this shit wouldn't be happening. Damn, what kind of double-edge sword was this?

A few minutes passed, and Sean was finally

successful at calming Torch down, which enabled him to throw a couple of questions his way. "Torch, I know you're probably not too fond of law enforcement, but right now we're the only ones who can help you get out of this situation you're in."

"Man, I don't need your help!" Torch interjected.

"Can you just listen to what I have to say first?" Sean tried to reason with him.

"Listen, dawg, you might as well take me to jail, because I ain't about to sit here and have a conversation with you like we're cool. I ain't got shit to say to you and nobody else."

"So you are telling me that you aren't willing to help yourself get out of this trouble?"

"Yeah, nigga, that's exactly what I'm saying."

"Well, do you realize that we can charge you with possession of a loaded firearm, brandishing a firearm, kidnapping, threatening a government witness, and threatening a federal agent?"

"I don't give a fuck about that shit! Take these handcuffs off me and I'll give you a reason to charge me with murder," Torch replied sarcastically.

"Well, if you wanna get fifteen to twenty years in federal prison, that's fine with me," Sean said. "Get this trash out of my face." Then I heard Sean instruct Agent Morris to take Torch to their central station and stick him inside a holding cell without a telephone.

"You can keep me from using the phone all you want, but that ain't gonna stop the word from getting out that that bitch back there is a snitch! So tell her to watch her back," Torch blurted out.

A few minutes later, the entire apartment had become quiet. That was my cue that the agents had taken Torch away.

Let the games begin!

Chapter 15

It's Do or Die

Sean walked into my bedroom after Torch was escorted out of the apartment. I was sitting on the edge of my bed looking spaced out. "Are you okay?" he asked me.

I turned my attention toward Sean. He was standing only two feet away from me. "I'm so fucked up in the head right now," I began to say.

"I can only imagine."

"I don't think you can. I mean, do you realize that I could've gotten killed a few minutes ago? If those other agents hadn't come when they did, he would've shot both of us."

Sean took another step toward me. "Let's not dwell on what could've happened. Right now we need to focus on getting that wire back on you so we can gather more intel and begin to put Bishop and his other boys behind bars."

"You have got to be joking, right?" I replied sarcastically. "One of Bishop's right-hand men just stuck a gun up to my head and almost dragged me out of this apartment and you still want me to wear that wire?"

"It's the only way. We can't turn back now."

"Well, I don't care what you say. I'm not putting that wire back on. That'll be a sure way to get a one-way trip to hell after Bishop gets word that I'm working with the feds."

"How will he find out? My men won't let Torch get his first phone call for another seventy-two hours."

I laughed. "And you think not letting Torch use the phone is going to keep Bishop from finding out what's going on? Torch is from Newark. And everyone around here knows him and knows that he works for Bishop. So all Torch needs is for someone to see him in handcuffs and Bishop will be notified immediately."

"No one will see him. The agents are transporting him in one of our trucks. And if this will make you feel better, we're taking him to our headquarters, not the city jail."

"Well, don't you think that if Bishop doesn't hear from Torch, he's going to think something is wrong?"

"That's where you come in." Sean said.

"And what does that mean?"

"It means that you're gonna cover for him. Tell Bishop he came by and before he left he got a phone call from a woman and told you that he's going to pay her a visit."

I shook my head. I was becoming more and more aggravated with Sean's plans by the minute. He didn't know Bishop like I knew him. Bishop was a very smart street cat. He saw bullshit from miles away. So I knew that if I'd tell him that bogus-ass story, he'd look at me all crazy. Torch never talked to me about his private affairs with women, so why would he start now?

"Listen, Sean, you're gonna have to come up with something better than that," I replied, and then I stood up. "Bishop will see right through that bullshit!" I continued.

I wasn't about to wait for Agent Sean to come up with a better plan. I left him standing in my bedroom and headed to the kitchen. The light inside of his head must've come on, letting him know that I wasn't coming back, so a few seconds later he decided to follow me.

I was getting a bottle of water from the refrigerator when Agent Sean finally joined me. I opened the bottle of water at the same time he looked at his watch. "We don't have much time, so I need to know where you put the wire."

I took a sip of my water and then I walked out of the kitchen and headed into the bathroom. Agent Sean followed me again. But before he attempted to enter the bathroom, I came back out with the wiretap in hand. "Here it is."

After he took the wire device from my hand, I asked him to excuse me and then I headed back in the direction of the kitchen. Agent Sean followed me down the hallway for the third time. "Are you ready to put this thing back on?"

I had my back turned to him while I was checking to make sure the front door was locked. Didn't want Bishop to pop up like Torch did. At least with the door locked, I figured it would give Agent Sean enough time to climb out of one of the windows in the bedroom or the bathroom before Bishop got in the house good enough.

"Look," I said immediately after I turned to face him, "I told you back when I was in the bedroom that I am not wearing that. Now, I'm not trying to give you a hard time, but I believe we can come up with a better solution, like hiding a wiretap inside of this apartment. Because this mess here isn't going to work," I pointed out.

"We don't have time for that. It would take a couple of our security analysts at least a few hours to get those bugs in place. And besides, we're trying to wrap up this case and serve our indictments in the next two to three days."

"Sean, I know you know what you're doing, but I'm telling you right now that if Bishop is trying to contact Torch and isn't having any success, then he's going to get really paranoid, especially since he now knows that his sister, Bria, was a snitch and Manuel's spot just got shut down. So if I say I was the last person to see him, Bishop might look at me weird. And I can't take any chances and wear that wire. It's a bad idea and it's a suicide mission on my part."

"Who says that Torch made it here to see you? If Bishop asks you if you've seen him, then all you have to do is tell him no."

"I don't know," I said, shaking my head. I didn't agree with anything Agent Sean had to say. So I took a seat on the edge of the living room sofa. He stood across the room from me, holding the wire device in his hand.

Sean's cell phone started ringing. He immediately took his phone out of the holster that was attached to his belt and answered it. "Agent Sean," I heard him say.

"How far away is he from the apartment?" he asked the caller.

"Will I have time to leave before he gets here?" His questions continued.

"Okay. I'll handle it from here. And don't call back. I'll call you," he instructed the caller, and then he disconnected the call. When he looked at me, I saw fear in his eyes. He didn't look spooked, but it felt like he was trying to warn me. So I sat there and waited for the inevitable.

"Bishop is on his way to the apartment. So you've got to find a place for me to hide," he finally told me.

Panic engulfed my entire body. I didn't know whether to stay put or get up and run. I knew the same situation that happened to Torch wouldn't happen to Bishop. Bishop was too clever. He possessed this type of wit that only street cats could get. And his level of treachery was beyond humane. When Bishop saw that he had an enemy in his midst, he didn't waste any time eliminating the problem. The thought of it made me want to die. I swear, if Agent Sean would take his government-issued pistol and shoot me right now, I'd be better off. But unfortunately he had another plan. So while Bishop was unlocking the front door with his key, Agent Sean yanked me up from the sofa and literally forced me to show him a safe place to hide.

The apartment had only four rooms—the living room, the kitchen, my bedroom, and that small room we use for storage, so finding somewhere to hide was nearly impossible. My heart felt as if it were about to burst from my chest cavity.

But thank God for a clear mind. I was a nervous wreck, but Sean was focused enough to find a small spot in the back of my walk-in closet. He had to literally stoop down with his back against the wall and remain perfectly still to prevent Bishop from ever finding out that he was there.

By the time I closed the closet door, Bishop had made it into the apartment and closed the front door behind him. I was nervous as hell, but I calmed myself down and met him in the hallway before he was able to come into the bedroom.

"I thought you had somewhere to be?" I questioned him.

"I do. But I decided to get Torch to ride out with me so he could watch my back. So I told him to meet me here," Bishop explained. And then he headed down the hall toward the bedroom.

"Where are you going?" I asked him. My nerves were shot. I swear if it weren't for Agent Sean having his pistol cocked and ready to fire, I would've turned around and left that apartment faster than anyone could imagine.

"What kind of question is that? I'm going in the bedroom," he told me.

I tried to swallow the imaginary pill that was

lodged in my throat, but it wouldn't go down. It was evident that he was going into my bedroom, so I rushed down the hallway to try to deter him from going into the closet. But before I could get into the doorway of the bedroom, he said, "I need some privacy, so go back into the living room until I'm finished. As a matter of fact, let me know when Torch gets here."

"All right," I said. And then I watched him close the door in my face.

I stood by the door of my bedroom to see if I could hear Bishop's movements. All the while, I prayed that he wouldn't go into my walk-in closet.

Several seconds later, I heard Bishop open up one of my dresser drawers, so I knew exactly what he was doing. I also knew that Agent Sean could see Bishop from his angle in the closet. I just hoped that he wouldn't blow his cover by jumping out at Bishop once he saw Bishop taking the dope from his stash spot.

But then again, I figured that maybe Sean would see the package and think that it was something else. Or maybe that was some wishful thinking on my part? Whichever way Sean tried to shift this situation, I prayed that he wouldn't put me smack-dab in the middle of it, because at the end of the day I wasn't going down for anyone. No way. Wrong answer.

A couple of minutes passed and then I heard

Bishop putting my dresser drawer back on its wooden track, and then he pushed it back in. And when I heard him close the drawer completely, I tiptoed away from the bedroom door. I rushed toward the kitchen to avoid being caught. He'd freak out if he caught me snooping around while he was trying to handle his business. I could see him screaming on me right now and calling me every name in the book. Not only that, he'd probably become leery of my ass too. And I can't have that. I've come along way with this cat. And I've got to get compensated before I tell him to kiss my ass.

"Lynise, has anybody been in here?" I heard him yell as he entered the kitchen. I saw the package of dope tucked underneath his shirt. It poked out just a bit around the stomach area.

"No, of course not. And what kind of question is that, when I'm the only one who's been here," I replied with the sincerest expression I could muster. I had to admit that he caught me off guard with that question.

"Because I smell a man's cologne. And it ain't nothing I'd wear," he continued.

I stood in the kitchen with my bottle of water in hand and said, "That's not cologne you smell. It's that new Febreze air freshener I bought a couple days ago," I lied. I crossed my fingers and hoped he'd believe me, because I didn't need another of the same episode that happened with Torch.

"Oh a'ight," he started off, and then he turned his attention to his wristwatch. "Damn, that nigga Torch ain't got here yet. He knows we gotta make this run in the next hour. I wish he'd bring his ass."

A few minutes later, Bishop took his cell phone from his pocket and began to dial a number. I knew he couldn't be calling anyone other than Torch, as they had important business to handle together. So I turned my back to Bishop and gave him his privacy. But I worried how Bishop would take it when he was not able to contact Torch. I needed this thing with Agent Sean and his obsession to bring Bishop and his whole crew down to happen as soon as possible. I had my life riding on this whole thing, so something or someone had better give up the goods before I flip the fuck out.

Immediately after Bishop dialed the phone number, he stepped outside and closed the door. I had no idea if he was about to leave, but I knew that he wanted more privacy. Before I could process my next thought, I heard a cell phone ringing. The sound was somewhat muffled, but I still heard it. And when I realized that the ringing came from one of the sofa cushions, I almost lost my damn mind.

Torch must've dropped his phone while the

agents were escorting him out of the apartment, and if Bishop walked back in and found out that Torch's cell phone was in this apartment, there's no way I'd be able to explain how it got here. So I sprinted over to the sofa and dug my hands down in between the cushions where the agents had Torch sitting, and lucky for me, I located it. My nerves were shot to pieces, but I managed to power the phone off just in the nick of time. As soon as I stuck the phone down inside my pocket, Bishop walked back into the apartment. "Did I hear a phone ringing in here?" he asked. He looked a bit puzzled. But I held on to my composure and told him that the ringing had come from the TV.

By this time I had taken a seat on the sofa. "Damn, well that cell phone sure sounds like Torch's phone," he commented, and then he locked the front door. I tried to act like I was engrossed in a movie on the TV, but it didn't work. Bishop had more to say. "Why the fuck this nigga ain't answering his phone? He told me he was about ten or fifteen minutes away and that he was on his way here. But I done got here before his ass."

I kept my eyes glued to the TV. I felt like if I looked at Bishop long enough, he'd know something wasn't quite right. And every so often, my mind would take me back to the fact that Agent Sean was hiding in my bedroom closet. I asked God a couple of times while Bishop paced the floor to make sure Sean remained still inside the closet, because the devil would surely come out if Bishop had his way.

Finally a commercial aired on TV, and by this time Bishop had taken a seat on the other sofa. He looked down at his wristwatch once again and said, "I can't believe this nigga hasn't gotten here yet. He knew we had something to do."

"Who's supposed to drive?" I asked.

"He is."

"Well, maybe he stopped to get some gas," I commented. I was trying to stay neutral in this whole thing. The worst thing I could've done to myself was act all paranoid. Bishop was real astute and would've seen through it the minute he sat down on the other sofa and got a good look at me.

Bishop looked at his BlackBerry once again. "Why the fuck he ain't answering his phone? He knew what we had to do."

"What is his phone doing after you call it?" I knew when Bishop called it, it went straight to voice mail because I was the one who powered it off, but I had to play the role.

Frustrated, Bishop said, "That shit keeps going straight to voice mail."

"Maybe his phone went dead," I offered. But my insides were boiling over. I just wanted

Bishop to come to the conclusion that Torch wasn't coming so he'd get up and leave. I was sweating bullets from my armpits. I felt that if Bishop didn't hurry up and leave the apartment, something else would go wrong.

Bishop sighed. "Yeah, you might be right. But then again, I know how that nigga is, and if I tell him to meet me, he's going to be there. So my gut is telling me something ain't right."

"Stop overreacting. I told you that he's probably just getting some gas. So I'm sure he'll be here soon."

"I understand all of that. But I gotta be somewhere at a certain time, and if he doesn't hurry up, I'm gonna have to hit the road alone," Bishop told me.

Thankfully the movie I was watching came back on. When I turned my focus back on it, Bishop got the hint and went outside. And as soon as he closed the door behind him, I let out a sigh of relief. Sorry to say, my exhale moment was short-lived, because in a matter of fifteen seconds, Bishop was right back in the apartment with me.

"I can't wait for this nigga another minute. But if he comes here after I'm gone, tell 'im I got the stuff and to meet me at the spot across town."

"Is that all you want me to tell him?"

"Yeah, 'cause after you say that, he'll know

what you're talking about. Oh, and by the way, I got my number changed."

"When did you do that?"

Bishop stood at the front door. "I got it changed a couple hours ago. So get your phone and lock me in when you see a 973-555-1212 number."

I reached for my phone. "When are you going to call me?"

"I'm gonna do it now while I'm walking back to the car," he replied.

"Okeydoke," I said, and then I turned my attention once again toward the TV. I had to pretend that my focus was on the television so he'd leave as quickly as possible. And guess what? It worked. After Bishop closed the front door, my phone rang and his new cell phone number appeared. I keyed in his name next to it and then I saved it. Immediately after that, I got to my feet and exhaled. There was nothing like having all of that pressure released from your entire body. I swear, if Bishop would've stuck around for at least another thirty minutes, there was a huge chance that I could've had a heart attack. I knew too much about everything involving Bria's disappearance, Manuel's run-in with the raid on his spot, Torch being arrested, and the indictment that would soon be served on Bishop and the rest of the group, so my cup was full. I'm surprised that I hadn't had a fucking nervous breakdown. There's no way a person could know all of what I knew and still have a sane mind. I knew one thing: if I didn't hurry up and get out of this environment, I may end up creating my own demise.

Constantly looking over my shoulders!

Chapter 16

The Clock Is Ticking

When I felt like Bishop had gone out of the neighborhood, I raced back to my bedroom and flung the closet door open. Agent Sean was standing when I laid eyes on him. Sweat was popping around his temples. He looked kind of flustered, so I stepped aside, giving him enough room to exit the closet. "Is he gone?" he immediately asked.

I exhaled. "Oh, my God! Yes, he's gone. But it feels like I'm about to have a fucking panic attack."

Sean grabbed me by the hand and led me to my bed. "Take a seat. And breathe in and out a few times and you'll be all right."

I sat and did the breathing exercises for a minute or so, and realized that I felt just a little bit better. While I continued his method to calm myself down, he pulled out his cell phone and made a call. "Hey, Amy, is he gone?"

"Yes, we're following him now. And we can tell that he's definitely in a hurry." I heard the female caller's response. The volume on Sean's BlackBerry was up very high.

"Well, if he gets way ahead of you, just fall back. Remember we can't afford to bring any attention to ourselves. He's already expressed that he believes that we're onto him, so again just be careful. And if by chance you lose him, then it's fine. Just come back to the apartment building and get back to your post."

"Okay. Got it," I heard her say, and they ended their call.

"I just got word that Bishop is long gone. So let's get back on track before he decides that he wants to return," Sean insisted.

He stood over me while I sat on the edge of my bed in deep thought. I was still trying to calm down my nerves. My mental state was in disarray. But that didn't matter to Sean.

"Come on, Lynise, the clock is ticking," he uttered, giving me a look of frustration.

The pressure was coming down upon me once again. But I stood my ground. "Sean, I told you I wasn't putting that wire back on. Now, if you want to arrest me and get me for obstructing justice, then do it, because right now I don't know if I'm coming or going."

Sean stood there for a moment. I could tell

he was feeling irritated, but at this point I couldn't have cared less. There was nothing he could do to me that hadn't already been done. Having lived in Virginia all my damn life, I'd been introduced to everything underneath the sun, from getting my ass whipped by disrespectful-ass niggas to doing time in jail behind some shit that had nothing to do with me. So nothing, and I mean nothing, Agent Sean does to me is going to penetrate this hard skin I have.

"I'll be right back," he said, and then he left the room.

I had no idea what he was about to do, so I waited for him to come back, probably after he'd concocted another one of his dumb-ass plans. "Hey, Amy," I heard him say, and that's when I figured out he had gotten the female agent back on the phone. I could tell he had gone into the bathroom, because I heard the echo after every word he uttered. "Do you think we can get a couple of the techs to come out to this apartment and set up some wiretaps?"

I couldn't hear Amy's response this time, so I waited for Sean to give me the verdict. "Okay. Well, call the office and put in a work order. We need this thing done like yesterday."

Once again the load was lifted from my shoulders. But there was no telling how long that feeling would last. It seemed like every other minute Sean had some bullshit story up his sleeve.

After Sean made his phone call, he came back in the room and gave me some bogus spiel. I listened to him harp on the fact that he was doing me a favor by putting wiretaps in the apartment. He could have talked to me until he was blue in the face, but I would've continued to stand my ground about not wearing that stupid wire.

In the end I got what I wanted and he got what he wanted, so it was a win-win for the both of us. The only person who lost out was Torch. I imagined he was spitting fire by now while he was stuck in a one-man cell. And he understood that it was all because of me, so I knew he'd give every penny he had in his stash to get his hands on me. I never wanted to imagine what they would do to me if they knew I was no longer on their side. It's a scary thought when you're in a dark place and there's no one around to help you. So to stay alive, I now realized that I needed to stay one step ahead of the feds and one step ahead of Bishop, because the clock was ticking.

Agent Sean was on his way out of the apartment, but he stopped in the middle of the living room floor and then turned back around to face my bedroom. I was still sitting on the edge of my bed. But I could see him from where I was. And when he began to head back down the hallway toward me, I tried to build up a mental wall, because I had a huge feeling that he was about to come out of his mouth sideways. I took a deep breath and braced for whatever he threw at me.

"Before I forget, tell me what was inside of that electrical-tape package Bishop took from underneath your bottom drawer."

I knew Sean was going to come out of left field. I also knew that he would question me about what Bishop was doing when he came into the bedroom and closed the door. I actually thought he was going to ask me this shit sooner than he did.

"How did it look?" I asked, trying to play naïve.

"It was a square package, about ten inches long and about four inches wide. And it was wrapped up in multiple layers of gray electrical tape."

"I can't tell you anything about that. Are you sure you saw him take something from underneath my drawer?"

"Yes. While I was hiding inside your closet I was able to see him through the slanted wooden plates on your door. So when he came into the bedroom I got a clear view of him removing the last drawer from the dresser. After he got it completely out, he turned the drawer upside down, took the package that was taped to the bottom of it, and then shoved the drawer back in place."

"Wow, you sure saw a lot," I commented.

"Yeah, I did. And what really peaked my interest was the fact that immediately after he got the package in his hands, he shoved it down into his jeans. And then he tried to cover it up with his T-shirt."

"Well, if you know all of this, then why are you asking me questions? I mean, it seems like you already have all the answers."

"You're absolutely right. But I need you to confirm what I just witnessed. So, you're saying you have no knowledge of what could've been inside of that package?"

"Yeah, that's exactly what I am saying. Bishop doesn't tell me anything."

"He didn't tell you about that drop you made to Manuel's house, but as it turned out, you were trafficking drugs," he replied sarcastically.

"Okay. So you got a point. But again, he doesn't tell me anything. I know you heard him when he told me to tell Torch to meet him at the spot. He didn't give me any more information than that. Oh, but he did give me his new cell phone number."

"Where is it? Give it to me," he demanded.

"It's 973-555-1212."

"Hold up! You're saying it too fast. Say it again, but this time say it slow." He pulled a pen and a business card from the inside of his jacket pocket.

I recited Bishop's new cell phone number

to Sean. And when he was done writing it down, he stuck both the pen and the business card back into his jacket pocket. "Do you know how many guns he has?" Sean wanted to know.

"Of course not. Since I've been in his company I've seen him with only one gun."

"What kind was it?"

"I don't know," I lied. I couldn't let him know that I knew anything about guns. I wanted to play the naïve role as much as possible. It was bad enough that he knew about my dilemma back in Virginia. So to add more fuel to the fire would take my criminal resume to a higher height, and that wasn't cool.

Sean gave me an expression like he knew I was lying to him. And quiet as kept, I was. But that was a lie, among others, that I intended to take to my grave. Agent Sean had already had me under lock and key with this investigation, so this was some information I had to keep close to my heart. Yes, I knew Bishop stashed his dope in my bedroom, but I refused to tell Sean about it. After Sean served the indictments on Bishop and his crew, I planned to rob Bishop for everything I could get my hands on, and that included the dope packages he stashed in the apartment. I vowed to take back everything I lost in all the relationships I had in the past. I was going to make Bishop pay for all the niggas who dogged me out. Now, I knew that my actions weren't fair, but guess what? Life isn't fair either.

Agent Sean wasn't too pleased with the answers I had given him. But it didn't matter to me. I knew how to play his dumb ass to the left when I needed to. He wasn't all that hard like he portrayed himself to be. So that's exactly what I did. But before he left the apartment, he instructed me to be out of the house by ten o'clock in the morning because his team would be by to install the wiretaps. "Stay gone for at least two hours. And make sure Bishop is with you. We can't have another episode like we did earlier," he said.

I thought I needed to get some rest after Agent Sean and Bishop left the apartment, but I was wrong. I don't know if it was my conscience or my intuition telling me that I needed to keep one eye open and the other eye closed.

When I looked at the alarm clock I noticed that it was a little after three a.m. Bishop never came back to the apartment, but he called and asked me if Torch ever stopped by. So of course I lied and told him he never showed up. The news definitely hit him like a ton of bricks and caused him to become more aggravated. I could also sense that he was worried too. But what was I supposed to say? That he came by earlier and that he snuck up behind me while I was having a conversation with Agent Sean? And that he heard us talking about me wearing a fucking wire so I could set them up? Yeah, that would be the day I lost all consciousness. And before I knew it, my body would be cut up into tiny pieces and thrown into an old Dumpster. And the crazy part about it was that no one would ever look for me or put out a missing person report. My own family wouldn't even come looking for me. Since I was a child, my relationship with them was screwed up. It seemed like everyone including my mom, my dad, and even my ex–best friend, Diamond, had it out for me. And the cats I had in my life weren't all that good to me either. If they weren't cheating on me, they were beating my ass. But then Bishop popped up in my life and acted like he was the best thing since sliced bread. And it turned out that he was a fraud just like everyone else. Who knew that he and I would get together and I would follow him all the way up north to start a new life, only to find out that he was being investigated by the feds and that he was about to go to jail for a very long time? So in the end it didn't matter that he was an asshole like everyone around me, because he wouldn't have been any good to me behind bars. I never did the prison visits or the pen pal thing. So I guessed my life would be just like it always had, *Fucked Up As Usual!*

I need an exhale moment!

Chapter 17

Taking What's Mine

Later that same morning was the time that Agent Sean and his team decided to plant the wiretap inside of the apartment. They left it totally up to me to keep Bishop busy for a couple of hours. Sean instructed me to leave the apartment around ten a.m., so I called Bishop around eight-thirty and complained to him about a stomach virus I had gotten overnight. My plan was to get him to think that I was so sick that I needed him to take me to one of the nonemergency medical centers in the area so I could get treated. When he answered his phone, it sounded like he had just wakened up. "Hello," he said.

"Are you just now waking up?" I asked.

He yawned through the phone. "Yeah, you

know I was up all night trying to handle my business and get in touch with Torch at the same time."

"What time did you finally get in bed?

"I got in the house a little after four a.m., but I didn't fall asleep until around five."

"Well, what time are you planning to come out the house today?"

"I don't know. Why? What's up?"

"I'm not feeling too good. I feel so nauseated when I stand up for a long time. And when I tried to put something in my stomach, it came right back up. I think I need to go to one of these nonemergency medical facilities so they can check me out."

"Well, there's one not too far from where you are. So why don't you get dressed and go?"

"I called you because I was hoping you would take me."

"Lynise, I am too tired to go anywhere right now. I've had only a few hours of sleep. So there's no way I'll be able to crawl out of this bed. My body won't let me."

I sighed heavily. "So you're going back to bed after you hang up with me?"

"That's the plan."

"Well, I'm too weak to drive myself anywhere. So I guess I'll wait for you."

Bishop remained silent for about twenty seconds and then he said, "Get ready. I'll be over there in an hour."

And before I could acknowledge that I would

do as I was instructed, Bishop disconnected our call. I started to take offense to it, but since I knew how tired he was, I left well enough alone.

Before I got dressed I called Sean and informed him that the plan to keep Bishop away from the apartment was still a go, but we would be leaving in thirty minutes, earlier than the appointed time. "That's fine," he said, "just make sure you stay on schedule. We got a lot riding on this wiretap."

"I know. Don't worry. I'll take care of my end," I assured him.

"Oh, did I tell you we confiscated one hundred thousand dollars from Torch's car?" Agent Sean asked.

My mouth fell to the floor. "You have got to be kidding."

"No, I'm not," he began to say. "After we towed his vehicle to our garage, I had my team search it inside and out. They found the money hidden inside a toolbox in the trunk of the car."

"Oh, my God! Bishop is going to freak out when he finds out that Torch is missing right along with his money."

"So you think that money belongs to Bishop?"

"Of course I do. Torch works for Bishop."

"Well, Bishop can say good-bye to that money, because it belongs to the Bureau now."

I almost got sick to my stomach listening to Sean tell me that they confiscated one hundred grand from Torch and now they owned it. What kind of bullshit is that? What about me? I think I ought to be getting a piece of the action. I am the one putting my life on the line. Shit! I swear, I wished I knew Torch had that money, because I sure would've snatched at least half of it for myself. I could've done some good shit with that dough. But now the fucking feds were probably going to invest that cash into some kind of dumb-ass tactical training program for their local office, which I find a waste of time and money. But hey, what could I do about it? The damage had been done.

Toward the end of our call, Agent Sean made me promise that I'd call him before Bishop and I headed back to the apartment. After I gave him my word, we said our goodbyes.

Like clockwork, Bishop was at the apartment all geared up and ready to take me to the doctor. I tried to play the sick role when he walked into the apartment, but sometimes it seemed like I was going a little overboard. He didn't make mention of it, but I could tell that he was anxious to get me there so the visit could be over and done with.

On our way to the car I noticed how deserted the parking lot was. Okay, granted, it was a weekday morning and most of the tenants were probably at work, but the neighborhood never looked like a ghost town before. As Bishop drove out of the neighborhood, I wondered where in the hell the federal agents were hiding out. There was no sign of them anywhere.

I looked at Bishop, and he seemed worried. I knew it had a lot to do with him not being able to get in contact with Torch, so I brought the matter up. "Have you talked to Torch yet?"

"Naw, his phone keeps going to his voice mail."

"Have you been by his house?"

"Yeah, I went by there twice. And I talked to his wife, and she hasn't heard from him either."

"Wow! That's crazy! She needs to get on the phone and call all of these hospitals around here. He's got to be in one of them."

"She already did it, and none of them has him in their computer."

"Has she called all of the jails in the area?"

"Yeah, she called all the precincts in and around Newark. And none of them had any record of him in their system."

"Well, where in the hell could he be?"

Bishop let out a long sigh. "If I knew, we wouldn't be having this conversation right now."

I turned my attention away from Bishop and watched the scenery from the passenger-side window as we passed by. I took into consideration that I wasn't down south where I was able to see acres of land filled with trees and green grass, so the picture I painted in my mind came with thirty-story buildings, some with tenants and some abandoned. As I thought about Torch's conditions, images of him pacing the floor of the holding cell inside the Federal Building came to my mind instantly. I even pictured him punching the walls with his bare hands as an outlet for the frustration he felt. From what I was told by Sean, Torch would be held in that very cell until the indictments are served and everyone has been picked up. But what if everyone isn't picked up in the time frame Sean gave me? Wouldn't it be unlawful for them to continue to hold Torch without giving him his one phone call?

I had no idea how the court system worked up here in New Jersey, but I knew that shit wouldn't be tolerated back in Virginia. Most of the cops and agents back in my part of town went by the books generally. So I couldn't tell you which way this situation would've gone. However, I was aware that everyone's Witness Protection Program ran the same. If you're working for the cats in suits, you're more likely to do whatever becomes necessary to get their job done. Just know that it comes with consequences, meaning life or death.

To get the heat off me, I indirectly pressed the issue about Torch's whereabouts. I had to make Bishop think that I was more concerned about Torch than being nosy.

"Have you thought about the possibility that the guys who kidnapped Bria could very well have Torch?"

After I asked Bishop the question I looked at him and waited for him to respond.

The first thing I noticed was how the veins in his neck popped up through his skin. And then I noticed how his eyelids kept blinking. I hadn't known Bishop as long as everyone else, but I knew I was pressing some sensitive buttons. So after much thought he said, "Naw, he ain't been kidnapped. Niggas ain't that brave to run up on him. The cats around here know that the niggas who roll with me aren't to be fucked with!"

"Well, why was Bria kidnapped? Isn't everyone around here aware that she's your sister?" I pointed out.

Irritated, Bishop snapped. "Look, stop asking me all these motherfucking questions. I'm not in the mood for this shit this morning. So let's drop it."

"My bad. I was only trying to help."

"You will help me by keeping your mouth closed."

Doing as I was told, I cut off all communication with Bishop for the rest of the ride to the medical center. It took tooth and nail to get him to bring me to the doctor's office, so God forbid if I got him so angry that he'd drop me off and leave me to fend for myself. Boy, Agent Sean would be livid if Bishop came back to the apartment sooner than expected and in turn forced the technicians to abort their assignment. I knew I wouldn't hear the end of that. My ass would sure be in hot water. And that would be too much heat to handle.

After a ten-minute drive, we finally made it to the nearest clinic. It wasn't your typical well-equipped private physician's office, but what would you expect in a slum part of Newark? The clinic was no bigger than a small store, and to make matters worse it was packed from one wall to the next with young chicks trying to get shots for the babies and niggas trying to get some medicine for their STDs. It was a sight for sore eyes.

When I first walked through the front door, I had every intention of turning around and walking back out, but when I thought about how Agent Sean would react if his investigation was compromised, I had a change of heart. I psyched myself into believing that the sooner I get him what he asked for, the sooner I could get out of his town.

Where did I intend to go? I couldn't say. But I did know that wherever I decided to go, it would be better than this place.

After I checked in at the front desk, Bishop and I took a seat in the waiting area. We hadn't been sitting for five minutes before Bishop's cell phone rang. The loud talking among the adults and the children crying influenced his decision to take the call outside. "I'll be right back," he told me.

I can't explain why, but I will say that I became nervous as hell after I heard his phone ring. It could've just been a call from his main lady, Keisha, for all I knew. But the fact that I had sold my soul to the devil made me paranoid about everything. Going against Bishop and trying to suck him dry is like starting war with another country. Bishop was nothing to fuck with. There was no in between with him. He was either hot or cold. And that's it. You can take it. Or leave it. And in this case, I had to take it, because it was all about Numero Uno!

Bishop stayed outside for thirty minutes, if not longer. I got up from my chair and peeked out the glass door a couple of times to see if he was still there. Naturally I became nervous when he made hand gestures as he talked to the caller over the phone. I didn't jump to conclusions about what he was discussing. I just assumed that it had something to do with Torch. Torch was a significant fixture in Bishop's life. Even though I'd known Bishop a short time, I knew he would call on Torch more than he'd call on Monty. From my understanding, Torch and Bishop were childhood friends like Diamond and me. So I knew he'd have a fucking heart attack if he discovered that Torch was in federal custody because of me. Boy, I would be one dead bitch! I believed Bishop would make me die a slower death than Diamond did. See, Diamond didn't mean anything to Bishop, which was why he got rid of her ass really quick. My situation would pan out much differently. Killing me would take time. Bishop would want to make me suffer because I betrayed him. He would probably tie me up and gag me so he could inflict pain on me. I could see him carving the skin away from my body like a chef slices a turkey. I could even see him pulling back the nail beds from my fingers or poking my face with the lit end of a cigarette until my face caught fire. I knew all this because I'd overheard him and Torch talking about how they massacred and tortured a nigga before they left to come to Virginia to avenge his brother Neeko's murder. We were all in the car driving north, and while this conversation went on I was supposed to be asleep. But all and all, I was playing possum.

Now, someone with a more drama-free life would've asked me why would I want to accompany this man and his boys to his hometown knowing all that I knew. And my answer would have been that, in some insane way, I was attracted to men who'd kill to protect their circle. It was a fatal attraction I had acquired since day one, and I wasn't afraid to tell the whole world about it.

Once Bishop finished his chitchat, he joined me back in the clinic. I could tell that he wasn't in the mood to talk, so I pretended to be engrossed in the magazine I was holding.

Thankfully, my name was called a few minutes after Bishop sat back down beside me. I saw the relief in his eyes when he heard my name. But he elected to stay in the waiting room while I saw the doctor. I was fine with that and assured him I wouldn't be much longer. And then I got up and left.

Time to act sick!

Chapter 18

Fake It Until I Make It

Icouldn't believe it. The Asian doctor I saw had me in and out of the examination room in a matter of fifteen minutes flat. When I emerged from the back of the clinic, Bishop jumped to his feet and walked toward the exit door before I got by half of the other patients in the waiting room.

It was evident that he couldn't wait to get out of there. I shared his sentiments, because I didn't want to be there from the start. But I'd had to come up with a good-enough reason to keep him occupied until Sean and the technicians installed the wiretaps inside the apartment.

As Bishop drove out of the clinic parking lot, I looked at the time on the dashboard and noticed that it was a few minutes after eleven-thirty. Sean initially instructed me to be gone for two hours, and since there were thirty minutes left from that two-hour window, I knew I needed to stall Bishop a few minutes more. "The doctor said I had a twenty-four-hour stomach virus and that I needed a few things like chicken broth and clear sodas to coat my stomach. He also told me to take an over-the-counter pain reliever like Ibuprofen. So could you stop by the nearest grocery store? I wanna get those things before you drop me back off."

"Yeah, a'ight," he replied, and those were the only words he uttered from his lips during the drive. When we arrived in front of the convenience store, he opened his mouth once to ask me if I wanted a ginger ale or Sprite. And after I told him I preferred Sprite, he exited the car.

After I saw him enter the store, I grabbed my BlackBerry from my handbag and dialed Sean's cell phone number. I knew I didn't have much time to talk over the phone, so I prayed that this call would be quick. Luckily, he answered it on the first ring. "Agent Foster," he said.

"Hey, Sean, it's me, Lynise," I replied.

"Are you guys on your way back?" he asked me.

"Yeah, we're at the convenience store about eight miles away."

"Okay, great timing. We're leaving the apartment as we speak."

"Good. Because I was about to have a panic attack thinking that we were going to come back too soon and Bishop would catch y'all in the apartment."

"Well, take a deep breath because that won't be happening."

"Where did y'all put the wires at?" I wanted to know.

"All over. So don't worry about anything. We'll be able to get all the intel we need if you get Bishop to incriminate himself."

"I already told you he's not gonna talk about his sister. He damn near cursed me out the last time I questioned him about her. So I'm not even going there with him on that subject anymore."

"What has he been saying about Torch? Has he brought him up to you?"

"No. But I said a few words about him."

"What did you say?"

"I asked him had he spoken with him yet, and he told me no. He said he called Torch's wife and she's looking for him too. Bishop also said that she's called every hospital and jail looking for him, so I got really nervous when he told me that."

"Don't worry about that. What's today?"

"What do you mean, what's today?" I was somewhat dumbfounded, not knowing where he was going with this.

"What day of the week is it?"

"It's Friday. Why?"

"When did we take Torch into custody?"

"Yesterday, Thursday."

"Okay, well, since we arrested him so late in the evening my guys at the Bureau made it their priority not to process him until after three p.m. today. And by doing that Torch won't be able to see the federal judge or make his first call until Monday. So we got this entire weekend to make this thing happen. And again, if you get us the information we need, we won't need you to go before a grand jury. Now, how does that sound?" he asked.

"It sounds good. That really takes a load off my shoulders. But look, I gotta get off this phone because I see Bishop at the checkout counter, so he's gonna be coming back to the car in a minute."

"Okay. Talk to you later."

A few minutes later Bishop returned to the car with a small bag. He got back in the car, handed it to me, and didn't say another word to me until we arrived back at the apartment. "Want me to carry that bag for you?" he asked.

"It's okay. I got it," I assured him.

Even though Sean had already informed me that the wires had been installed and that they were packing up to leave, I still felt the jitters in my stomach the moment Bishop and I exited the car. Bishop walked ahead of me. I was supposed to be sick, but I tried to walk fast enough so it wouldn't look obvious that I was trying to catch up with him. Sorry to say that it didn't work. Bishop sped ahead as if he knew something had happened inside of the apartment and he needed to confirm his suspicions.

I watched him as he entered the apartment. I was only a few steps behind him, so I entered four seconds later. He walked into the bathroom immediately after I closed the front door. I went into the kitchen to put my things away, and when I was done I took a seat on the living room sofa and powered up the TV. I picked up the remote and sifted through the channels. Meanwhile, Bishop made a startling discovery.

"Lynise, come here for a minute," he yelled from the bathroom.

Hearing the tone of his voice naturally made me feel uneasy. I was a nervous wreck, and at that moment I wanted to ball up and roll into a fucking corner. But knowing that I was in this situation and had nowhere to run, I dragged myself to see what it was he wanted. And when I got to the bathroom door, he stepped to the side so I could walk by him.

"Who's been in here?" he asked.

"No one," I told him as my heart picked up speed.

"Well why the fuck is the toilet lid up?"

I looked down at the toilet and then I

looked back at him. The wheel in my mind was spinning. Bishop knew that I'd never be in the house and use the toilet while the lid was up. So I had to come up with a good explanation as to why it was up. He knew he hadn't done it, because he hadn't been here since yesterday when he came looking for Torch. In my mind, I knew the guilty party was among the group that Sean escorted in here to wiretap the apartment, but I couldn't tell Bishop that. So I said, "It's up because I left it up after I spit up all my food I ate last night. And do you know that this is your second time asking me who's been in this apartment? Do you think I'm really that damn crazy to let somebody come in here?"

Bishop searched my face as if he didn't believe my response. So I pulled out the reverse psychology card and smiled. "Now are you going to answer my question?" I continued.

Bishop wasn't budging. He was too serious for words, so I cracked a joke hoping he'd lighten up. "Okay, you got me!" I began to say. "I forgot to tell you I had a penis." I burst into laughter while I rubbed my stomach. I still had to play the role that I was trying to get over the stomach virus, so technically my stomach should have been tied in knots.

Unfortunately, Bishop didn't think my little joke was funny. In fact, he acted as if he was turned off by it, because instead of commenting he looked at himself in the bathroom mirror and then he left me standing in the bathroom. I was shocked that I didn't get offended when he walked out on me. I guessed it had a lot to do with the fact that I had so many other things eating away at me. I felt like, the less time he's in my face, the better.

The only thing that did bother me was that he was being overly paranoid. I guess he had the right to be, since he lost Neeko back in Virginia and then got back here to New Jersey to find out about the issue with Bria. Not to mention he was about to have a fucking baby if he didn't find Torch. So things around him were crumbling. I just hoped that I got out of the way before the entire thing blew up in his face.

After Bishop walked out of the bathroom, I turned and looked at myself in the mirror. It was shocking to see my facial expression. I looked totally in fear. I mean, I actually looked like I had come in contact with a fucking ghost. And to see how my chest reacted to my heartbeat was even scarier. Having Bishop demand that I do shit for him on one end and then having Agent Sean demand that I do shit for him on the other end was detrimental to my well-being. I couldn't tell you whether I was coming or fucking going, but I could tell you that it had to stop one way or another.

Before I left the bathroom, I took inventory

of everything around me just to make sure nothing else was out of place. Agent Sean or his technicians already had Bishop questioning me about the fucking toilet lid being up. I couldn't have any other slipups.

If it ain't one thing, it's another!

Chapter 19

Who Can I Trust?

Bishop's cell phone was like his lifeline. Every damn time I turned around, his face was glued to it. I lay back down on the sofa to get some rest, and he was in the kitchen getting himself a bottle of water when his BlackBerry started ringing. He quickly took the phone from his jean pocket and answered it. "I hope you got some good news for me," he said to the caller.

This time around I couldn't hear the caller's voice so, I couldn't determine whether it was a man or a woman. But then Bishop said, "Damn, Monty, this city isn't that big, he's gotta be around here somewhere," and I knew who he was talking to. I also knew he was talking about Torch. I figured he had Monty looking under every rock in the streets just in case somebody whacked Torch and left him in a ditch somewhere. I turned down the volume on the TV just a little bit so I could eavesdrop on his conversation some more.

"There ain't so many places he could be," he began. "The last time I talked to him he said he was on his way to Lynise's place, but he didn't ever make it. So whatever happened to him happened after he got off the phone with me," he continued, and then he fell silent once again.

I wondered what Monty was saying on the other end. I knew Agent Sean wondered what Monty was saying on the other end as well, since the entire apartment was wired.

"Look, check it out," Bishop said. "Somebody knows something. A grown-ass man doesn't disappear into thin air just like that. So I need you to put the word out to everybody on the streets that I'm willing to pay ten grand for any information that would lead us to his whereabouts, whether he's dead or alive. 'Cause if we find him, we'll be able to find out where my hundred grand is."

Listening to Bishop tell Monty that he's willing to pay ten grand for information regarding Torch made me wonder if he'd get desperate enough to go up on that price. Shit, if he gave me fifty grand I'd make up an anonymous name and tell him where Torch was. And right before he'd get a chance to talk to

Torch and find out that I was the reason why he was behind bars, I'd be long gone. Crossing the border into Mexico would be my best bet. But then again, that wouldn't be a good idea, since the drug cartels in that country are fighting against each other.

A good move for me would be to go back down south to Miami or something. No one knows me there. And who knows, I may even win the heart of a good man this time around.

Meanwhile, as I pondered the likelihood of me moving farther down south, Bishop said something to Monty that piqued my interest.

"Monty, I can't have you pounding the streets looking for him yourself. Call Chrissy and see what she can find out, because I'm gonna need you to go by my house and tell Keisha to give you that package out of the freezer. After you get it, I need you to drop it off to the spot over on Sixth Avenue," he told Monty, and moments later he disconnected his call.

I thought he'd come into the living room where I was to check if I was all right. But he stayed in the kitchen, and I heard him dialing another number. He remained quiet as a mouse, and I assumed that he was waiting for the other caller to answer their line. And then suddenly he said, "Monty is on his way to the house. So when he gets there, give him that fish stick box in the back of the freezer."

I figured she gave him some lip service and became somewhat belligerent, because after he yelled at her and called her a dumb bitch, he hung up on her. I did a double take when I heard his outburst. He was livid. And I refused to have him take his aggression out on me, so I turned the volume back up on the TV and acted like I hadn't paid him and his act any attention.

Not too long after he hung up on her, he finally joined me in the living room. I looked into his face and noticed how tired he looked. He also looked worried. I couldn't imagine the pressure he was under. But I had an idea. "Are you all right?" I asked him.

"Naw, I ain't all right. But I will be as soon as shit start coming together for me."

"Whatcha getting ready to do?" I probed.

"I ain't getting ready to do shit. I'm thinking about going in the bedroom to take a nap. But I'm afraid that if I go to sleep, I may miss an important phone call."

"If you want me to, I could wake you up."

"Nah, I'm good. I'ma hop back in the car and take a ride across town. So I can clear my head," he told me.

"Bishop, if you're tired then you really need to get some rest. Remember you said you only had a couple of hours of sleep last night. So please take a load off and go lie down." I tried to encourage him.

It seemed like I was pulling tooth and nail, but he finally agreed to lie down for an hour. I knew time was of the essence and the sooner I got Bishop to talk while he was in the apartment, the sooner Agent Sean and the rest of his team could get enough evidence to do their sweep and arrest all parties involved.

Before Bishop headed off toward the bedroom, I had an idea and ran it by him. "I know you don't like talking about certain things, but have you thought about the possibility that Torch might've skipped town on you? I mean, you did say that he had a lot of your money in his possession."

"Yeah, I thought about it."

"I'm glad you did. One hundred thousand dollars is a lot of money."

"Yes, it is," he commented.

"Well, I just wanted to make sure that you're being open-minded, because there's a lot of things that could've happened to Torch."

"Yeah, you're right. And that's why I'm giving away reward money. Somebody's seen him and knows where he's at."

"I'm sure they do too," I agreed.

"Thinking about that shit makes my head hurt, so I'm going in the room to lie down. If anybody comes over here looking for me, come get me before you let them in."

"Okay," I replied, and then I watched him as he started toward my bedroom.

Bishop closed the bedroom door so he could have total peace and quiet while he rested. I stayed in the living room and managed to keep my composure knowing all that I knew. Anybody with this much shit on their mind would probably have a fucking nervous breakdown. But I was acting like a real champion and dealing with all of the unnecessary drama that was thrown onto my plate. I couldn't wait until all of this shit was over so I could go on about my merry way while Bishop handled the pressures of losing not only Neeko, but Bria and all the money he made off someone else's blood. When I thought about how nice he was to me in the beginning, and how he took matters into his own hands when my life was hanging in the balance, I came to the conclusion that it was all just a front. Even though he helped me back in Virginia, he had me here making me pay off my debt to him. Now tell me he isn't a sneaky motherfucker. *Ole bastard!*

I hate niggas!

Chapter 20

Another Bites the Dust

One hour into Bishop's nap his cell phone rang. When he answered it I jumped up from the living room sofa, where I was watching television, and raced to my bedroom door just so I could eavesdrop. I remained perfectly still. I even held my breath a couple of times because it sounded like I was breathing too loud.

Alarmed, Bishop said, "Keisha, whatcha mean the police just left there? What did they say to you?"

I couldn't hear what Keisha was saying to him, but I knew that whatever it was, it wasn't any good news. So while he listened to her, I heard him moving around the bedroom. I couldn't take the chance of him opening the door and seeing me standing on the other side, so I rushed back into the living room and pretended to watch TV. Thank God I listen to my intuition, because immediately after I sat down my bedroom door opened.

When Bishop walked into the living room, he gave me a blank stare. I wanted so badly to ask him what was wrong, but I decided against it because I knew I'd start an unnecessary war with Keisha if she heard my voice on this end. I just sat back and waited for him to get off the phone. I figured then he'd tell me what was going on.

"First off, you need to calm down. They ain't got shit on you. Because if they did, they would've arrested you and you wouldn't be able to talk to me right now. So just sit tight and I'll be there in a minute," he told her, and then he fell silent to give her a chance to speak.

Forty seconds later, he said, "Well, did they say anything about Monty?"

I couldn't quite figure out what Keisha was saying, but I could tell by Bishop's facial expression that Monty was in deep shit.

"Keisha, just lock the fucking door. And if they happen to come back before I get there, do not open the door." After he gave her his final instructions, he hung up his cell phone.

"I'll be right back," he told me, and raced toward the front door.

I got up from the sofa. "You're gonna leave

just like that and not tell me what's going on?" I complained.

Bishop stopped his tracks and turned to face me. "Come on now, Lynise, I don't need another headache. I got too much shit on my mind."

"And I understand that, but when I hear you talking to Keisha about the police, and how they've talk to her, that makes me a little worried. Especially when I know that you and her share the same place."

"Look, I understand what you're saying, but I'm the type of man that prefers to keep his woman in the dark about his business affairs as often as possible. I don't want you to be concerned with what's going on at the house me and Keisha share. Just worry about this place, and everything will be fine."

"Well, is there anything you would like for me to do while you're gone?"

"I'll call you and let you know, so keep your phone right by your side," he replied. And within seconds, he was gone.

As soon as Bishop closed the front door I grabbed my BlackBerry, retreated to my bedroom, sat down on the edge of my bed, and I wondered why the police questioned Keisha.

I had to admit that I was pretty disturbed by the fact that Bishop wanted to keep me in the dark about the situation with Keisha. I had my suspicions, and if my suspicions were correct, that phone call Keisha made to Bishop had everything to do with Agent Sean and his investigation.

Curiosity had me locked in a death grip. There was no way I was going to sit in this apartment and wait for Bishop to call me back with some news. I needed to know what was going on right now. Since I had Sean on speed dial, I rushed to get him on the line. After he answered his phone and gave me the Agent Sean spiel, I went into question mode full force.

"What's going on? Bishop's other girlfriend named Keisha just called Bishop acting all frantic, saying that the police were at her house asking her a lot of questions. So my question to you is, were those police officers she was referring to you and your boys?"

"As a matter of fact, it was. After we heard Bishop instructing Monty to stop by his house and have Keisha hand him that package from the freezer, that information gave us and the local police a reason to initiate a traffic stop. At that stop, the local cops told him they had pulled him over because he looks like a murder suspect who is on the loose. So of course they asked him for his identification, and then they made him step outside of the car. But he refused to do that and sped off. Luckily, we had a couple of agents in the area monitoring the traffic stop, so they were able to stop the vehicle and apprehend Monty before he caused a major traffic accident."

"So, do you have him in custody now?"

"Yes, we do. I have two agents transporting him to our headquarters as we speak."

"Did y'all find a whole lot of drugs on Monty?"

"I can't say exactly how much he had. But I assure you it was plenty."

"So, did she see you guys arrest him?"

"No, she didn't."

"Well, why did she call Bishop all hysterical and tell him he needed to come to their house?"

Before Agent Sean could answer me, I heard his phone beep, indicating that there was another caller trying to get through to him. "Hey, Lynise, I'm gonna have to call you back."

"Oh, okay." I said.

When Agent Sean hung up with me to take the other call, I felt like a dog left out in the rain. I mean, could you believe it? Right when he was about to answer my question, another call comes through. How freaking convenient.

I was about to explode because I wanted to know what was going on. Not only had Bishop left me in the dark, so had Sean. And it didn't feel good at all.

I dropped my cell phone down on the bed and got up so I could take a bathroom break. When I took the first step, I noticed an identification card face down on the floor, but half of it was hidden underneath the right end of my bed. I reached down to pick it up, and when I turned it over, my heart skipped a beat.

I never fathomed that I'd find Bria's driver's license in my damn bedroom. A weird and horrible sensation came over me. I knew that I hadn't taken her ID card from her, so Bishop had to have done it himself. "Oh, my God!" I said aloud after the thought of her actually being dead entered my mind.

Even more unsettling was the fact that I had a talk with Bishop after I saw Diamond's Virginia driver's license in his wallet at the mall. I will never forget when he told me he took her ID so it would be hard to identify her body without it. He even admitted that it was a game for him to walk around with his victim's ID cards in his wallet. "I also do it for the enjoyment. I mean, it ain't like they need it," I remembered him saying once.

I thought it was really weird and gross of him to do that, but hey, who was I to judge him? He was a nigga from New Jersey who obviously had not an ounce of sympathy for the dead. I mean, come on. Who kills someone and then takes their fucking driver's license? That shit was crazy! And here I was playing fucking wifey to a nut job. I knew one thing: I had the evidence that probably proved that Bria was dead. Now, I can't say how I planned to present this big piece of evidence to Sean, but I figured I'd come up with something.

On my way out of my bedroom, I slid Bria's

driver's license into my back pocket. But then I stopped and reentered my room. Something was eating away at me, and it had to do with my bottom drawer. I hadn't heard Bishop tamper with it today, but it nearly drove me crazy to find out whether he had something hidden in his secret hiding spot. So, just like I always did, I slid the drawer out very careful, and when I removed it completely from the dresser I turned it over, but there was nothing there. I felt like a balloon that just got popped. The hopes of my finding his dope stash came crashing down. I swear, I was so disappointed. My intention to find his dope was solely based on the fact that I knew he was about to be taken down by the feds, so I needed some travel and living expenses. And if I got a hold of his drugs I could sell them wholesale and come off lovely, depending on how much I take. But hey, something's got to give, because the hourglass has almost run out.

Meanwhile, my cell phone rang. I didn't bother with putting the drawer back into the dresser for fear that my caller would hang up if I took too long to answer. So I got on my knees, reached on my bed, and grabbed my phone. I noticed it was Bishop, and I answered it.

"Lynise, this bitch is trying to set me up! I swear, I'ma kill her!" he screamed through the phone. I imagined his eyes bloodshot red, with the veins around his temples flared up. I even pictured him releasing spit from his mouth every time he uttered a word.

"Kill who? What's going on?" I managed to say after his unexpected outburst.

"That bitch Keisha called me and told me to come to the house because the police came there and asked her a whole bunch of questions. Well while I'm driving, I decided to take the back way into my neighborhood just to be on the safe side. So, about two blocks over from my house, I noticed the same mother-fucking crackers that was following us down the turnpike sitting in their truck waiting for me to pull up."

"How do you know that they were the same guys?"

"Because I remembered the license plates. And you know I don't forget a face."

"Oh, my God! This is crazy." I commented. Who would've thought that Keisha would turn on Bishop just like that? I mean, she dated him long before I came into the picture, so for her to jump ship was a huge indicator that she had no loyalty for him from day one. I thought I was a sellout chick for handing Bishop over to Agent Sean like I did. But now I see that Keisha was more heartless than I was.

"Are you serious?" I said, trying to sound surprised.

"You motherfucking right I'm serious. That bitch called me to come to the house so them crackers could arrest my ass. But they just don't know that I ain't no dumb-ass nigga. I'm always on the lookout for sheisty motherfuckers like that bitch! So they better hide her ass, because if I ever get a chance to run up on her, I'ma kill her motherfucking ass. And it's gonna be a slow and painful death."

"I told you she wasn't shit!" I commented, trying to point fingers. I needed him to see Keisha for who she really was in an effort to shift the negative attention on her. I figured if Bishop focused on Keisha, then I would be the least of his worries.

"Oh, it's all right. She's gonna get what's coming to her. But check this out," he said, "I'm gonna need you to go into the back of the freezer and take out that bag of frozen spinach, and inside of it you're gonna find some valuable items. Now, once you get 'em, I want you to put them into your purse. Then I need you to go into the bedroom closet, but take a chair with you because you're gonna have to reach your hand up into the left side of the ceiling and pull down a Nike shoe box. And inside that shoe box is some money, so I'm gonna need you to put that in your purse too and be ready to come outside when I get there."

"When are you coming?"

"I'm coming now."

"If you saw those white guys waiting outside your other house, do you think it would be wise for you to come back here?"

Bishop didn't respond, so I assumed he was in deep thought. But then after sixty seconds of pure silence, he said, "Yeah, you might be right. So come back up to that clinic we went to earlier. I'll be inside waiting for you."

"When should I come?"

"You need to leave the house now."

"Okay."

I didn't see this coming!

Chapter 21

The Hunt Is On

My heart moved faster than my feet after I hung up with Bishop. But I knew it was very important for me to calm my nerves and focus on the task at hand. Bishop gave me specific instructions about how he wanted me to execute his plan of attack. The first place he instructed me to go was the refrigerator freezer, so I headed into the kitchen.

While I was en route to the kitchen, it dawned on me that he changed his stash spot for his drugs. And I wondered why he did that. Well, whatever his reason was, I hoped it had nothing to do with me. Influencing him to have second thoughts about me was not a good look. I needed to remain the good girl around him so there wouldn't be any mishaps.

Immediately after I entered into the kitchen, I searched the back of the freezer and retrieved the spinach bag from where Bishop told me it would be. It felt weird holding this bag. And after I pulled out the contents, I realized that the aluminum foil wrapped package had to be worth a pretty penny. I wanted to open up the package to see exactly what I could be working with, but I decided against it. I figured since I was pressed for time, it would be better to do it later.

My next destination was my bedroom closet. Bishop instructed me to grab the Nike shoe box hidden in the ceiling because it contained money that belonged to Him. He didn't mention the amount of money, but the urgency in his voice gave me the impression that it had to be one hundred thousand dollars or better.

I knew it was a little unorthodox, but I said a silent prayer to God, asking Him to let the money in the box be enough money to take care of my needs. I also prayed that He'd help me find a way to get away from Bishop so I could walk with this money free and clear. I failed to mention to God that I had intentions on keeping the dope I found. I decided against it because I knew it would be the wrong thing to mention in a prayer. Besides that, I knew from childhood how God operated. He did things on His time, not mine, so I made sure I told God I'd start going to church when I settled down in a new state. Now, I couldn't tell you if God heard my prayer, but I knew that I had a sincere heart when I prayed to Him. So I guess I'd see where he'd take me from here.

Getting mentally ready to pull Bishop's money from the ceiling of the clothes closet had its effects on me. One part of me wanted to take it down and run as fast as I could, and the other part of me became afraid that if I managed to take it, I'd somehow get caught. Bishop was a very resourceful guy. He knew a lot of people, and he was known for reaching out to them if he needed them to eliminate a problem for him. To make a long story short, Bishop wasn't to be fucked with. But hard-headed me took chances. And today I wanted to see what I had to look forward to.

"Come on, Lynise, it's time to get this thing done so you can be on your way," I mumbled very quietly as I climbed onto the chair and balanced my weight on it. A few seconds later, I pushed up on the square ceiling plate and then moved it enough to the side so I could reach my hand into the small space. Once the space was open, I reached up and touched the shoe box. I grabbed it and then turned my body around enough and threw the box onto my bed. Once that was done, I slid the ceiling plate back over and then I jumped down to the floor.

I'm not lying when I say that I felt a slew of different emotions. And to say my heart was beating extremely fast was an understatement.

I was a basket case. It felt like I was on the verge of having an anxiety attack. Knowing I had possession of Bishop's dope and money made me question my next move. But knowing how much I had would give me a sense of direction. So I sat down on the edge of my bed, and while I held the Nike shoebox in my hand my damn cell phone rang. It startled the hell out of me. When I snatched it up from the other side of my bed, I noticed that it was Agent Sean trying to contact me. Annoyed at the fact he called me at the wrong time, I sucked my teeth and then I answered his call.

"Hello?"

"Lynise, why did you tell Bishop not to come back to the apartment?"

"Because I got scared when he told me he wanted to kill Keisha. Do you think I want him to find out that I was turning on him too?" I explained. I knew Agent Sean heard our conversation, so I had to keep it real and tell the truth.

"What's the name of that clinic he took you to earlier?"

"Why? Are you going there to arrest him?"

"Yes. We got Monty in custody right now. We got him right after he picked up that package from Bishop's house. And we also have Keisha, and she has decided to cooperate with us, so we really don't need you anymore."

"Does that mean I'm free to leave town?" I asked. The sound of Agent Sean giving me my walking papers was like music to my ears. I was finally getting what I wanted and there were no strings attached.

"Yes, you're free to leave. But not until you give me the contents of the packages Bishop instructed you to get from the freezer and your bedroom closet."

Shocked by Sean's demand, I almost lost my cool. I had endured all of life's obstacles and here goes this bastard trying to take what was due to me. Was he crazy or something? I wasn't about to hand over shit! This money was as much as mine as it was Bishop's, and he was the one who made it through blood, sweat, and tears. So did Sean think I'd let him confiscate it so he could give it to the federal government? No way! I don't think so. He'd better come up with a better plan than that.

"Look, Sean, I know you heard our entire conversation, but it ain't like you think. The package I found in the freezer was a small roll of money wrapped up in aluminum foil. I can't tell you how much it is because I haven't had a chance to open it. And the shoe box in the closet has money in it too. But I don't know how much is in there either," I lied. I knew how the feds worked. If I had told him there was some dope in the freezer, he could've played me like a fiddle. This place was in my name, so there was no way I'd give him a package of dope that was hidden inside of my apartment. A conspiracy charge was written all over that, and I wasn't interested in wearing that charge.

"I'll tell you what, you stay at the apartment. My agents and I are going to the clinic to meet up with Bishop. When we're done with him, I'll be by there to get the money."

"Okay," I replied. But I had no intention of being here when Sean arrived. I had plans to pack my things and be out of here in the next ten minutes. I was going to take the car Bishop gave me and drive it as far as Maryland, and from there I planned to jump on the train and head farther south.

At the end of our phone conversation, I provided Sean with the name of the clinic I had visited earlier. But I made him promise me that he would sway Bishop into believing that I hadn't given him the location of the clinic and that it came from them bugging his cell phone. After Sean agreed to do just that, we said our good-byes.

Immediately after I hung up with Agent Sean I threw my BlackBerry back on the bed and then lifted the lid on the shoe box. "Oh, my God!" I said once again while I sifted through the stacks of one hundred dollar bills. There were exactly seven stacks. They were bound with three thick rubber bands. And from the looks of it, each stack was worth ten grand, but I wasn't too sure, so I took one of the stacks of bills from the box and counted it.

I went through the stack and found one

hundred of the one hundred dollar bills. The grand total came to ten thousand dollars. And since there were seven stacks, I figured I had seventy thousand dollars. It wasn't the amount of money I had expected, but I'd make it work.

Don't count my chips!

Chapter 22

The Safe House

I tore my apartment apart trying to pack the more important things I'd need to travel with. With only seventy thousand dollars in cash and a package of dope, I knew I'd need to plan all of my steps wisely. Seventy thousand dollars wasn't a lot of money, but it filled the void. And I decided that it would do me some justice since I came into this bullshit-ass relationship with nothing in the beginning.

Once I gathered up everything, I sat down on my bed again and remained very still. And that's when I realized how quiet it was inside my apartment. It was so quiet that it felt kind of weird. It was almost like the quiet before the storm. But I felt ready to tackle anything. That included Bishop, whether he'd believe it or not. I found myself in the middle of a bitter war between Bishop and the feds. They wanted him extremely bad. It was bad enough that they had to use Keisha and me as his weakest link.

Bishop already knew Keisha had jumped ship and sold him out to the feds. But when he found out that I sold him out too, I was sure to get death threats as well. I just hoped that I'd be too far out of his reach that he wouldn't ever run across me again.

Now with everything packed and ready to go, I decided at the last minute to leave Agent Sean a brief letter about how scared I was to stay inside of the apartment and that I was leaving behind the two thousand dollars I found. I ended the letter by saying that I appreciated everything he did, but that I feared for my life; therefore I felt it would be safe for me to go. The letter was only one page. Short and sweet. And once I felt it was complete with everything Agent Sean needed to know, I placed it on top of the kitchen table, along with the money I intended to leave, and then I headed back into my bedroom to grab my bags so I could leave this place indefinitely.

On my way back into my bedroom, I realized that I still had Bria's driver's license in my pocket. I had no intentions of taking it with me, so I took it out of my pocket, wiped off my fingerprints, and then hid it inside a pair of Bishop's Timberland boots that were left in the hall closet. When Agent Sean brings his team in this apartment to do a thorough search for evidence that would perhaps bring them closer to Bria's whereabouts or how she died, I knew finding her ID would give them a lead. And once that was done, I knew it was time for me to make my getaway.

With my bags in tow, I got to the front door and before I opened it I turned around and took one last look at the apartment. I knew I'd remember the good times I had here. I also knew that I'd remember that incident where I got roughed up by those dumb-ass niggas Bishop had instructed to come here. But all and all it would just be memories, and they'd forever be stored in the back of my mind. So, after I took a mental picture, I grabbed the doorknob and opened the door.

I thought I would've been ready for what was on the other side of the door, but when I pulled the door open far enough to see that I had company, my fucking heart sank. I nearly fainted when I saw Agent Morris and a female agent standing outside my door. What in the hell was I going to do now? There I was standing in the entryway of the front door with my travel bags in hand and a handbag filled to the rim with Bishop's money and his fucking dope, but I couldn't tell them that. Sean told me to stay at the apartment while he handled the situation with Bishop and then he'd come here immediately thereafter. But that's not what I did. I totally went against everything he instructed me to do and came up with my own plan. I figured that if I waited here long enough, I'd be putting myself in harm's way. I mean, who's to say that they'd be able to catch Bishop? For all I knew he could've been testing me to see if I'd play him like Keisha did. And who's to say that Agent Sean really had intentions to let me go free and clear? It was all a big gamble. And I was caught directly in the middle of it.

Can you believe this shit?

Chapter 23

What's Gonna
Happen Next?

I stood at the front door before Agent Morris while his female colleague stood next to him. Both of these white folks gave me a suspicious look. And before they started questioning me, I beat them to the punch and started the dialogue myself. "Oh, my God! Y'all scared me."

Agent Morris spoke first. "We're sorry about that. But we're curious to know where you're on your way to?"

I hesitated for a moment to think of a good explanation. And the only thing I was able to come up with was, "I wasn't going anywhere. But I was going to the car to put my things in there." And even though I tried to be sincere with my response, Agent Morris wasn't buying my story. He threw a monkey wrench in my plans, and I was about to pull out my fucking hair.

He stepped forward and pushed me back into the apartment. "No, that's not gonna happen. Agent Sean Foster instructed Agent Wise and me to come over and provide you with protection until they apprehend Bishop."

"You've got to be fucking kidding me! I don't need any protection," I snapped as he pushed me backward.

"No, we're not kidding. And yes, you do need protection," Agent Morris commented after he and Agent Wise entered the apartment.

I stood in the middle of the living room floor with my travel bags in hand, and I didn't like this picture I saw at all. There was no question in their minds that I wasn't too happy about them being here. So after Agent Morris locked the front door, I said, "Can you tell me how long I've gotta wait here before I'm able to leave?"

"I'm not sure, but as soon as we hear something, you'll be the first to know."

I sucked my teeth and stomped away from them. "This is some bullshit!" I replied sarcastically. I was so mad that I could've cursed those two agents out and not cared less what they thought about me.

"Agent Foster said you had some money for him. So, where is it?" Agent Morris asked.

By the time his question registered in my mind, I had walked back into my bedroom and dropped my things on the bed. My first thought was to give him a hard time, but then I said to myself that I wouldn't be helping my situation by being an asshole, so if I wanted to win their trust and play them at their own game, then I'd have to turn this thing around and use it for my benefit. "It's in the kitchen." I finally told him.

After I told Agent Morris where the money was, I heard him go into the kitchen to retrieve it. The other agent did a tour of the house. I suspected she did this to make sure we were the only ones inside the apartment. A few minutes later Agent Morris appeared at my bedroom door. For the first time I got a really good look at this guy, and I had to admit that he was a very handsome man. He was clean cut, but he had some swag about himself. Dressed in the normal suit and tie uniform, he wanted to know where the shoebox was that the money was stored in.

The Nike shoebox was on my bed, so I handed it to him. "Anything else you need?" I asked.

"No, I think this will be it for now," he told me, and then he walked away from the door.

Now, even though I was inside my apartment it sort of felt like I was caged in a cell. I mean, I literally had the feeling that I was being held against my will. And I didn't like it one bit. How dare these motherfuckers come in here and rain on my parade. Were they insane? I had all the right in the world to leave and go on about my business. But Sean threw some shit in the game and found a way to come in the back door on my ass. And the crazy part about all of this is, he knew he was sending these agents over here to babysit me, but his slick ass failed to mention it over the phone. I mean, I had been straight up with him, so why in the hell hadn't he done the same?

Getting the shitty end of the stick!

Chapter 24

Damn Federal Agents

Twenty-five minutes passed, and I heard one of the agent's phones ringing. Then I heard Agent Morris talking. "What do you mean he's not there yet?" I heard him say.

I was watching TV in my bedroom, but I was more interested in hearing his conversation, so I grabbed the remote control and turned down the volume. "No, he hasn't been here." Agent Morris continued to talk. And then he said, "I don't think he has, but hold on, let me go and ask her." Seconds later, he appeared at my bedroom door. "Excuse me, Lynise, but has Bishop tried to call you?" he asked me.

"No, he hasn't. My phone hasn't rung since the last time he called," I told him.

Agent Morris got back on his cell phone

and relayed the message to the caller. I suspected that it was Agent Sean, because he mentioned in an earlier conversation that he and a couple more agents were going to head over to the clinic and wait for Bishop to get there. But, after hearing this call, I'm forced to believe that he hasn't run into him as of yet. "Is that Agent Sean?" I blurted out.

"Yes. He's saying that he's at the clinic, but Bishop is nowhere in sight," Agent Morris said.

It was definitely a shocker to hear that Bishop hadn't gotten to the clinic yet. And not to jinx myself, but it wouldn't surprise me if he got there and spotted the feds posted up and left. "Well, I don't know what to say. He said he was going there. So maybe he changed his mind," I said.

Agent Morris spoke with Agent Sean for another minute or so and then he hung up with him. But less than one minute later, my cell phone rang. And my heart started pounding instantly. I knew it was Bishop before I looked at my phone. He had my number, so this was a scary moment for me. Both agents ran into my bedroom the minute they heard my Black-Berry ring. "Is that Bishop calling you?" Agent Morris asked me.

I looked down at my phone. "Yeah, it's him," I managed to say. My heart was beating uncontrollably.

"Answer it before he hangs up. But put it on speaker," he instructed me.

"Hello," I finally said. I tried to act as cool as possible. I couldn't afford to bring any suspicion upon me. Bishop was already a leery man. He trusted absolutely no one, especially after what Bria did to him. So I had to play this thing right.

"Where the fuck you at?" he screamed through the phone.

I was so at a lost for words. I didn't know what to tell him. So I looked at both of Sean's watchdogs for their assistance. "Tell him you're getting ready to leave the apartment," Agent Morris whispered.

"I'm getting ready to leave the apartment," I finally said.

"What are you fucking stupid or something? Didn't I tell you to meet me?" he spat.

"Yeah, but I was trying to pack up some clothes, so that took a little of the time," I explained.

"Did I tell you to pack up some fucking clothes?" he roared.

"No."

"Well, why the fuck are you wasting my time, Lynise? I'm trying to get the fuck out of Jersey and you're fucking around with my shit. Getcha ass out of the house now."

"Ask him will he still be at the clinic?" Agent Morris whispered.

"Did you still want me to meet you at the clinic?"

"Hell, naw! I left that place a long time ago. Niggas kept looking at me strange at that joint, so I dipped," he explained. "Meet me at the outlet mall. Go to the food court and I'll meet you there."

"Ask him what kind of car he's driving," Agent Morris whispered once again. But this time his words came out a little louder and unfortunately Bishop heard him.

I tried to muffle my phone, but it was too late. "Who the fuck is that talking?" he flipped out.

"It ain't nobody. That was the TV you heard." I tried to cover it up.

"You're a motherfucking liar, bitch! I know what I heard! You're trying to get me locked up like that other bitch! But I got something for y'all asses!" he screamed.

Immediately after he went on his ranting spree, the phone went dead.

I swear, I hadn't ever been so terrified in my life. I thought Duke's ass was crazy when I was fucking around with him. But Bishop got more serious problems that Duke. This damn man just threatened my life, and I was definitely not okay with it. So I looked at Agent Morris and said, "Thanks for putting me on his fucking hit list!" Then I got up from my bed and left my bedroom.

Both agents followed me down the hall. We

all ended up in the kitchen. "Don't worry about him. We have the best agents working on this case, so you're perfectly safe with us."

I grabbed a bottle of water from the refrigerator and laughed at him. "You should be a comedian. Because that shit you just said was funny as hell."

"Listen, Lynise, it's all right to be worried. But I promise you, you're gonna be fine," he continued.

"I find that hard to believe, especially when we're dealing with a motherfucker who killed his own sister because she ratted him out. He didn't give a damn about her after he found out she was compromising his business. He didn't care that they slept in the same bed when they were kids. So do you think he'll spare my life just because I fucked him a couple of times? Hell, naw, he sure ain't! He's going to hunt me down like he does everyone he sets out to kill. And then he's going to go into attack mode. Now I want you to remember that when he comes looking for me."

After I gave both of those dummies my speech, I went back into my bedroom. Agent Morris followed me down the hallway while Agent Wise stayed in the living room. He tried to give me his little pep talk, but that shit was bogus. That shit he was saying didn't make any sense. I tried to block him out, but I couldn't, so I said, "Please stop wasting my time, because there's nothing you can say that's gonna make me think any different. I know how Bishop is. I spent a lot of time with him when we were in my hometown. I've seen the treacherous shit he's done to people first-hand, so I don't wanna keep hearing you tell me that everything is going to be all right, because it's not. So, let's face it. I'm fucked! End of story!"

"Would you prefer that we put you in Witness Protection?" Agent Morris offered.

"Hell, naw! Are you crazy?" I spat. "Y'all should've left me alone and let me walk out of that front door and I wouldn't be in this fucked-up situation."

"I'm sorry. But I was only going by orders."

"Fuck them orders! They ain't worth the paper they were printed on," I said after I sat down on my bed. I was livid to the point that I would've swung on Agent Morris if he was close enough to me. It was obvious that he didn't know what the hell he was talking about. I knew what time it was. I also knew that it was a matter of time before he'd try to collect his money, his dope package, and me.

My life is in shambles!

Chapter 25

Can You Say Psycho?

Agent Morris got Agent Sean back on the phone after Bishop screamed on me and gave me the dial tone. I heard him tell Sean about the conversation Bishop and I had. He also expressed his concerns for my well-being. He told Sean how Bishop threatened me and that they needed to get me out of this apartment. I couldn't hear Sean's response, but I could tell by Agent Morris's expression that it was favorable. "Okay, we'll be ready when you get here," Agent Morris told Sean.

I was front and center during their chat, but I needed to know the specifics, so I asked Agent Morris for their plan.

"Agent Foster is en route, and as soon as he

gets here we're going to transport you to a secure location."

"What's gonna happen after that?" I questioned him.

"I'll let Agent Foster brief you on that when he gets here."

"Why do I have to wait for him to get here before I find out what y'all gon' do with me? Now see, that's some bullshit!"

"Agent Foster heads this investigation. So we have to wait to see how he wants to handle this situation."

Listening to Agent Morris blow smoke up my ass was beginning to piss me off. I knew he had clout among the other agents, so why was he playing games? This was my life hanging in the balance, and all these two dummies wanted to do was walk around here like they had broomsticks stuck up their asses.

After hearing enough of the lies Agent Morris was telling me, I got up and excused myself to the bathroom. I had to take a dump real bad. But I held out all this time because I didn't want to blow up the bathroom while they were here. Not to mention, I had a thing for privacy when I'm doing number two. I guess the privacy wagon went out the window the moment those two agents walked through my front door.

"I'm in the bathroom if y'all need me," I announced. Neither Agent Morris nor Agent

Wise acknowledged that they heard me, so I closed the door and handled my business.

I sat down on the toilet and went straight into thought mode. I wondered how long they were going to detain me. I also wondered about the possibility that I may not come out of this thing alive. The thought of that alone scared me to death, but I had to be real with myself to be able to see the bigger picture. So believe me you, the writing was definitely on the wall.

Five minutes of bathroom time would generally do it for me, but after I took care of my business, I washed my hands in the bathroom sink and then I stood there and stared at myself in the mirror. I was a very attractive woman, but it sure looked like I had aged a few years in these last couple of months. I believe that my circumstances surrounding my involvement with Bishop had taken its toll on me. The only way I'd be able to reclaim my sanity is by getting out of here as quickly as possible.

While I was still in the bathroom, my entire apartment shook. It felt like we were experiencing an earthquake. With the combination of a loud *BOOM* and the rumbling, I also heard Agent Wise scream, and fear engulfed my entire body. I tried to figure out what was going on on the other side of the bathroom door, but I couldn't make sense of it. One part of me wanted to stay in the bathroom where I might be safe, but then I decided that if it were an earthquake or a bomb, I needed to get out of here. So I grabbed the doorknob and snatched the door open. When I stepped out into the hallway I couldn't believe my eyes. Agent Morris and Agent Wise weren't anywhere insight, but there was a fucking old beat-up car sitting in the middle of the living room. It became obvious that someone deliberately drove it into this apartment. But when I looked at the driver's side of the car, there was absolutely no one behind the wheel. After seeing this, I became pretty alarmed. "Agent Morris, where are you?" I yelled.

"I'm over here," I heard him reply. But it was barely audible. And when I looked in the direction from which I heard his voice, I saw him in the kitchen buried underneath some of the rubble that came from the crash. So I ran to his rescue and helped him get up from the floor.

Immediately after I helped him to his feet, I noticed that he suffered mild bruises to his face. But he was more concerned about Agent Wise than his cuts and bruises. "Where is Agent Wise? Is she okay?" he asked me.

"I don't know. I heard her scream while I was in the bathroom. But when I came out here, she was nowhere in sight. And the driver of the car ain't nowhere in sight either."

"Are you sure?"

"Yes, I'm positive. But I know Bishop had something to do with it. He knew I was here because the car he gave me was still parked outside, so to shake me up, he made this happen."

"Come on, let's look for Agent Wise and then we're gonna hurry up and get out of here," Agent Morris said.

Agent Morris and I walked toward the living room. It was only a few feet away, but we had to step over a lot of debris before we could get there. I stumbled a couple of times, but Agent Morris kept me from falling.

"You better be careful," he warned me.

But I wasn't too worried about falling, I just wanted to hurry up and find the other agent before something else happened. For all we knew, Bishop could've been waiting for us to come outside to blow our fucking heads off. He also could've had those two cats who roughed me up standing outside to do me in as well. Bishop had unique ways of carrying out his death sentences. The people he preyed on never knew the exact time they'd take their last breath. All they knew was that their life would end. What a fucked-up way to live in the final hours of your life.

He's the fucking devil!

Chapter 26

Finally Getting Some Closure

Agent Morris and I searched through the rubble and finally saw Agent Wise. The devastating part about finding her was that she was dead. She had gotten run over by the car. We could see only part of her face, and it was saturated with her blood. Luckily she was facing the opposite direction. Her eyes were open, and I didn't think I'd be able to handle looking at her head-on.

Agent Morris immediately radioed Agent Sean, because he lost his cell phone among the debris. As he communicated with Sean, I ran back into my bedroom to get my things, because I knew it would be a matter of minutes before we got out of here. "We're about two hundred feet away from you, so stay put," I heard Sean tell Agent Morris.

"Copy that," Agent Morris replied. Soon he was at my heels. "Come on, we've got to get out of here."

I grabbed my things I had packed earlier and followed Agent Morris to the front door. Several seconds later, Agent Sean appeared with five other agents. It was one woman and four men. All of them, including Sean, were dressed in military-issued fatigue gear; bullet-proof vests inscribed with FBI; and the heaviest, most deadly artillery one man could carry in their arms. They looked like they were ready for war.

Sean grabbed me by my arm. "Come on, let's get you out of here."

I swear, this was the first time that I can truly say that I was happy to see his ass. And I was convinced that he would risk his life to save mine. He was geared up and ready to serve and protect.

A few of the neighbors stood outside while Sean and two other agents escorted me to the car. Local police even joined the party. "We're taking you somewhere safe," he told me.

"Okay," I replied.

When Sean helped me into the exact same black Suburban that followed Bishop and me down the New Jersey Turnpike, I shook my head. Who would've thought that I'd be traveling in it after Bishop noticed it on the Turn-pike and it was parked a couple of blocks from the house he shared with Keisha? Strange things tend to always happen.

While I sat inside of the truck, both of the agents guarded the truck from the outside. The windows were tinted so no one was able to see what position I was sitting in. "Do you have everything you need?" he asked me.

"Yeah," I said.

"Well, hold tight and I'll be right back."

"Can you please hurry up? 'Cause I can't stand to be out here another minute."

"Don't worry, I'll be right back," he assured me, and then he ran back toward the apartment.

I looked around the surrounding area and saw how most of the neighbors were migrating toward my apartment to see what all of the commotion was. I also watched as Sean, several police officers, and the other agents were inspecting the old car that smashed in the wall of my living room. Moments later, I watched as the city tow truck service arrived on the scene. Agent Sean said a few words to the tow truck driver and then he walked away from the truck. From that point, the tow truck driver proceeded to pull the car out of my living room.

Before he was able to extract the car from the apartment, Sean, four police officers, and the other two agents had to lift the car up so the tow truck driver wouldn't pull Agent Wise's body with it. Only after they struggled for ten minutes was the car finally removed.

Immediately after Agent Wise's body was retrievable, a coroner arrived, bagged up her body, and then they took her away. I didn't know her, but watching the coroner take her body was sad, because I could've very well taken her place. I just hoped that she didn't have any kids. It would be a miserable day if she did.

A few more minutes passed, but it seemed like time stood still. The crowd outside of my apartment grew larger by the minute. The agents and the police used yellow tape to secure the crime scene. It felt as if I were watching an episode of *CSI*. But even with the horrific scenes of that crime drama, I wasn't ready when Sean came back to the truck with more grim news.

After he climbed into the backseat next to me, he closed the door and said, "We just found Bria's body in the trunk of that car. And it looks like she's been dead at least two days."

I heard the words "Bria's body," but it took a few minutes before it registered in my mind. And when it finally did, I was completely taken aback. But I needed to know more. "Was she shot?"

"She was wearing a blindfold, and it definitely appears that she died from a gunshot wound to the head. So whoever shot her did it execution style."

"Whatcha mean 'whoever did it'? We both know that Bishop did that shit! That crazy motherfucker killed his own fucking sister. Now, how fucked up is that. I swear, I hope y'all give that son-of-a-bitch the death penalty when you catch his ass."

"Listen, we're gonna need you to help bring this joker down. Now, Keisha has already agreed to help, and since you're already on board we need to get you out of here right now and take you somewhere safe until we take him into custody," Sean said.

"Well, I'm ready," I assured him.

"So, you know, we're taking you to a Witness Protection Program."

"But, I don't wanna go in Witness Protection. I already told Agent Morris I wasn't feeling that. People that are snitching go into that program, and I'm not that kind of person. I was forced to help y'all. And look where it got me."

"Okay, listen, not all snitches go into that program. That program is for your protection. It's government funded, so we can use all the resources to make sure nothing happens to you."

I sat there with my arms folded and thought about what other options I had. And I came up with absolutely nothing. I did have Bishop's dope and sixty-eight thousand dollars. So, after all this mess is over with, I'd be well equipped to go on my merry way.

Once I was able to ponder on this situation I finally told Sean I'd go to the program, but I made him promise that as soon as Bishop was locked up, I'd be free to go. He agreed, and then we shook on it. But before he got back out of the truck he looked at me and said, "I'm glad you agreed to get protection, because when we looked in the trunk and saw the garage bag, it had a note taped to it that said, 'Lynise this will be you next.' "

Shaking with fear, I said, "Oh, my God! Are you for real?"

"Yes, I am. And that's why it's important for you to get into the program so what happened to her won't happen to you."

"Look, I've heard enough. Can somebody get me out of here right now?" I asked nervously.

"I'm gonna get Agent Paxton and Agent Morris to transport you to a safe location in just a minute," he replied.

After he gave me the rundown, he slid back out of the truck and pulled Agent Morris to the side. Seconds later, I saw Agent Morris coming toward me, so I knew I was about to be out of this place.

It's real in the field!

Chapter 27

No Way Out

Agent Morris got in the passenger side of the truck, and Agent Paxton drove. It felt good to be getting away from the apartment, but these dumb-ass cats thought I was going to be around for the long haul. No sir! Not me! I swear after all this shit is over, I'm getting missing in action. And once I get rid of the dope, I should have enough money to last me as long as I lived modestly and stayed underneath the radar. For now, I intended to keep my money and my plans a mystery. It's about Lynise and Lynise only.

"Where exactly are you guys taking me?" I asked. I figured since I was going into hiding, why not find out where they were taking me? I mean, it was my life that was on the line, and I felt like who better to look after it but me?

"We're taking you to a secured location called the safe house," Agent Morris answered.

"Is that like a house y'all got hidden in the woods or something?"

"I see you watch a lot of TV," Agent Morris commented.

"Yeah, I love the shows *CSI* and *In Plain Sight*," I replied, and then I turned my attention to the high-rise buildings as we passed them. "How far away is this place? Because it'll be a bummer if we gotta drive more than thirty miles."

"You shouldn't be worried about where we're taking you or how long it'll take us to get you there. Everything we do is confidential. But I will say that the place is safe and secure. And no one will be able to find it."

"Can you at least tell me if y'all are taking me out of the state?" I continued to probe.

"No. You're staying within the city limits. And once Bishop is picked up and prosecuted, then you'll be able to leave and go wherever you want," he answered.

Agent Morris kept giving me the runaround about where they were taking me, so I left the whole thing alone. I wasn't the type of chick to beg anyone. No way. He got me confused with somebody else.

During the rest of the drive the agents talked

amongst themselves, so I went into thought mode. I couldn't help but wonder where they were going to house me and how long I was going to be there. Finding out this information would help me figure out how to make my escape plan and how long I would need to come up with one.

Finally after a thirty-five minute drive, Agent Morris told Agent Paxton he had to use the bathroom. "Pull over to the Exxon gas station," he said.

"Yeah, I gotta take a leak myself," Agent Paxton told him.

"Well, I'll go first, and when I get back I'll stay here and let you go," Agent Morris insisted.

"Let's do it," Agent Paxton said, and then he parked the SUV next to one of the gas pumps.

I sat in the backseat and watched Agent Morris walk to the men's restroom, which was inside of the station. The sun was shining bright, and it seemed as though everybody was outside. I looked around to my left and saw a cute little Volkswagon Passat. It was white, and it looked like it had just been driven off the showroom floor. The chick behind the wheel parked it at the gas pump next to ours. When she got out of the car, I immediately knew that she was a stone-cold gold digger. She looked like she was Hispanic and black. Her hair was very long, but she wore it up in a ponytail, and she definitely had the body of a video vixen, minus the butt pads. I watched her as she removed a McDonald's bag and a drink cup from her car and threw it into the trash can next to her pump.

When Agent Morris came back outside, this young lady caught his eye. He got her attention by saying something to her, and after she looked up she smiled and stopped everything she was doing. I watched them as they walked toward each other. I made a comment to Agent Paxton about Agent Morris flirting with the woman. "Check out Agent Morris flirting with that young Spanish hottie," I commented.

"Where?" Agent Paxton asked.

"To your left." I replied.

Agent Paxton turned and saw Agent Morris talking with the woman. "He's not flirting with her. That's Chrissy. She's one of our linguist specialists," Agent Paxton said.

"Did you say Chrissy?" I said, because for some reason that name rung out to me.

"Yeah, why, you know her?" Agent Pax asked me.

Before I answered him I thought back to the time I spoke with a Chrissy from Bishop's phone. And I remembered Bishop talking to Monty about a Chrissy. But could this be the same Chrissy? "Naw, I don't know her. But I do know somebody with the same name," I finally replied.

"We all do," Agent Pax commented.

"So, what exactly does she do?" I wanted to know.

"She's the best translator in our office."

"Oh really?"

"Yes, she speaks like four or five different languages."

"Wow! That's hot!"

Minutes later, Agent Morris decided to join us. But instead of climbing back into the SUV on the passenger side, he walked up to the driver's side with Chrissy in tow. Agent Paxton rolled down his window. "What are you doing on this side of town?"

"My mom lives near here, so I decided to come out here to visit," she told him.

I swear, when she started talking I nearly pissed in my pants. This was the exact same chick I talked to on Bishop's cell phone. She had the same fucking squeaky voice. But how was it that she was involved with Agent Morris? I was completely at a loss for words. I was really confused and had no idea what to do.

"Today is definitely a nice day to take a drive," Agent Paxton assured her.

"Tell me about it," she commented. And then she said, "So, where are you guys on your way to?"

But before either one of them could respond to her, I interjected by saying, "Don't tell her! She's working for Bishop."

Agent Paxton turned completely around in his seat to get a good look at me while Agent

Morris peeked his head into the driver's side window. When Agent Morris opened his mouth to say something to me, both agents got their heads blown off. Agent Morris and Agent Paxton's brains were splattered all over the front seat and the windshield, and some their blood and flesh plopped on me as well. I was in complete shock. And I screamed as loud as I could.

After she took both of these men out, she pulled on the back door handle and tried to open it. Lucky for me, it was locked. "Somebody help me!" I screamed.

I saw at least five people next to their cars, but no one wanted to come near the truck. I did see a lady get on her cell phone, so I assumed she was calling the police.

"Somebody please help me! She's trying to kill me!" I continued to scream. I needed some fucking help. I figured that if these people weren't going to risk their lives to save mine, then they'd at least call the cops for me.

After three failed attempts to open both back doors, Chrissy tried to shoot the windows out, but she couldn't get them to budge. When she finally figured out that they were bulletproof, she stuck her gun inside the driver's side window and aimed it at me. She pulled the trigger, and I ducked down behind the seat, but that didn't prevent me from getting hit. The bullet went right through my left shoulder. The feeling of that bullet burning through my skin was unbearable. And I knew that if she got the chance to shoot me again, I wasn't going to make it. But thank God, she'd almost emptied the clip on both agents and the windows, because when she finally got to me, she only had one bullet left.

With the combination of frustration and hearing the police blaring their sirens, Chrissy hopped back into her car and sped off. I swear, I never felt so relieved.

Minutes after the cops and the paramedics arrived, I was carried out of the truck and placed on a stretcher. Right before they put me into the ambulance, I made sure they grabbed my purse and laid it beside me. I was in very bad shape, but that didn't alter my judgment in any way.

Finally arriving at the hospital, the paramedics pulled up to the emergency dock. When they rolled me out the back of the ambulance, they placed the stretcher on the ground, and that's when I got a strange feeling that someone was watching me.

So while they rolled me toward the entryway, I lifted my head as much as I could, and when I looked toward the parking lot, I saw this man who looked just like Bishop sitting behind the wheel of a parked car. My heart did summersaults. But at the same time, I wondered if I was seeing things. So I closed my eyes, and when I opened them back up, I took a second look, but the car was gone. Now, was my mind really playing tricks on me, or was Bishop lurking out there and waiting patiently for the perfect time to take me out? I couldn't answer the first question, but I knew he wanted me dead. And he wouldn't stop at nothing until it was done.

Thank God I'm still alive!

A gunshot wound . . . witness protection . . . a stint in a safe house . . . this isn't what Lynise Washington planned for herself when she moved to New Jersey with Bishop, a money-making gangsta. She thought he'd take care of her for life, until too much drama turned the tables. Now Bishop wants Lynise dead, and he'll use every resource he has. Too bad for him she's back in Virginia, primed for revenge—and this time she's playing on Team FBI. But when she and Agent Sean Foster start feeling each other, they incite suspicion—not to mention jealousy from the safe house's queen bee. Lynise isn't sweating it, though. With the explosive information she's packing, the agents need her at least as much as she needs them. And Lynise isn't planning to take one for the team, much less cave in to Bishop's wrath—even if she has to take matters into her own deadly hands . . .

A master manipulator is no match for a
killer in national bestselling author
Kiki Swinson's thrilling new novel
THE SCORE
On sale now!

Matt

A huge boulder was barreling toward me when a sound like thunder caused me to stumble and fall. But the boulder didn't catch up to crush me. Instead, I jerked out of my sleep and heard the thunderous sound again.

BOOM! BOOM! BOOM! That's when I realized I was no longer dreaming.

My heart was racing while my brain struggled to connect the sound with its source. Scared as hell, I forced my eyes open to the loud noise coming from somewhere in the condo. I tried to lift my head, but could barely move. The pain that shot through my skull from just opening my eyes was unbearable. It felt like somebody was standing over me, hitting me on the top of my head with the pointy part of a hammer. The noise came again. After being fully awake for a few minutes, I realized it was coming from the front door. I reached into my nightstand drawer for my gun.

"Oh shit," I croaked, barely able to move my dry, cracked lips. My mouth was so parched, it felt like I had swished a cupful of sand around and tried to swallow it. I was experiencing a cross between a bad hangover, the day-after effects of an ass whooping, and a bad case of the flu.

BOOM! BOOM! BOOM!

Damn. Whoever it was, they weren't going away or giving up. I cocked my gun. Then I heard the familiar high pitch of Yancy's voice. My shoulders slumped and I put the gun down on the nightstand.

"Matt! Lauren! I know y'all fucking in there!" If Yancy's screaming sounded that loud to me and I was in the back of my condo, I could only imagine how it sounded to our neighbors. This bitch was really wearing out the little bit of patience I had for her. This side-chick was horrible at playing her position.

I tried to gather up enough strength to stand up from the side of the bed, but it wasn't easy. "Awww fuck," I groaned. Not only was my head throbbing with pain, but I felt completely off. The room was on tilt. This was crazy, because I hadn't had a hangover in years. And from Ciroc? Nah, I wouldn't feel this fucked up from that mild-ass drink.

"Lauren?" I mumbled. "You here?" I struggled to move my pounding head so that I could look around the room. "Bae?" I called out to her. No answer.

"Maybe she ran out for a minute," I said under my breath. But why wouldn't she have woken me up? It suddenly dawned on me that we had business to take care of, hence the reason Yancy was pounding on the door like a madwoman. Speaking of which . . .

BOOM! BOOM! BOOM!

"Matt! Lauren! I'm not fucking playing! Open up this door!" Yancy. Again.

"Fuck!" I huffed.

I squinted at the cable box, and it read 4:55 p.m. I swiped my hand over my face and shook my head. I couldn't have possibly slept all fucking day.

"This bitch," I rasped. I gripped the side of the bed for support and slowly got to my feet. I almost fell backward. That is how bad my equilibrium was off. I felt like somebody slipped me a fucking roofie. I ain't never felt like this from no damn Ciroc.

I lumbered down the hallway to the condo door, barely able to lift my feet. I yanked opened the door to find crazy girl Yancy looking like a maniac on the other side. Her eyes were bugged out and had dark rings under them like she hadn't slept in days. Her hair was wild on her head. She had the illest look on her face too. Scary as hell.

"Why the fuck are y'all playing games with me?" Yancy barked as she bulldozed her way inside. Shit, she slammed into me so hard, I almost fell flat on my ass.

"What are you talking about? I was sleeping. Lauren must've gone to run some errands," I growled. "Fuck is you out here banging like the gotdamn police? You making it real hard to have a chill button around your ass."

"Run some errands? You let her leave? You can't be that stupid, Matt," Yancy spat. "Why would you let her leave without you? You really think she just went to run some fucking errands? I've been coming here since early this morning, banging on the door. I have been sitting outside and I haven't seen her come or go."

At first her words didn't quite sink in. "Wait. What?" I asked. I felt dazed.

"You heard me. I've been here since like ten this morning. Banging. Sitting outside. I left and came back. Started banging again. You just now hearing me? There's no way Lauren was here this morning and left."

I moved my head left to right, trying to shake off the fog that seemed to be looming over me. I looked around the living room and nothing seemed out of place. Then I checked the key hook and noticed that Lauren's car keys were gone.

"Let me call her," I grumbled. "Because you bugging right now. You mad paranoid and shit. I told you she probably ran out for a reason. Damn."

I slowly walked back to my bedroom to get my cell phone. Of course, stress-box-ass Yancy was hot on my heels like she was going to miss something. She was mumbling and grumbling, but I wasn't trying to hear her.

I picked up my cell phone from the nightstand on my side of the bed. As I dialed Lauren's number, I watched Yancy peek into our master bathroom, walk over to Lauren's vanity, snoop on her nightstand, and finally walk over to our closet. She was like the fucking feds on a search warrant, I swear.

"It's going straight to voice mail. Maybe her battery died. I'm sure she will be back in a few," I told Yancy. Even though I was trying to act like I believed that Lauren's battery had died, something in the pit of my stomach was telling me I might need to be worried. Lauren carried her phone around like she needed it to live, so she never let that shit go dead. I was still playing it cool in front of Yancy though.

Yancy squinted at me, folded her arms across her chest, and tapped her left foot impatiently. "Matt, she's gone. I bet you she's fucking *gone*," Yancy said calmly, taking a break from her panicky octaves.

"Nah. Where she gon' go? I'm all that she knows. Lauren ain't got the heart to leave me. You ain't gon' understand what I have with her, but I know she can't stand to be without me," I said confidently. But as the words left my mouth, I didn't know if I even believed that myself.

"You was all that she knew before we fucking stole three million dollars! I bet you that bitch is gone and I bet you even more that she has the fucking money too!" Yancy yelled, her face turning all sorts of shades of red. She started fidgeting her legs like she had to take a piss. "Matt, where did you put the money?" Yancy asked with panic lacing her words. "I want to see the fucking money. I want to see that shit right now, Matt. Where is it?!" she pressed.

"It's in my fucking safe, Yancy," I retorted. I walked over to my closet and stepped inside. My entire body was cold. My head was pounding. I wasn't up for this bullshit.

"It's probably gone," Yancy taunted from behind me. "Every fucking dime is probably long gone. That bitch got us. I'm telling you she took it."

I didn't know if she was trying to convince me or herself that the money was gone.

My jaw rocked, and I bit down on the skin inside my cheek. It was all I could do to keep myself from turning around and knocking Yancy's ass out. She was getting on my nerves.

I pushed my shoe box collection out of the way and moved the clothes I had blocking the wall safe. Nothing looked out of place to me. I punched in the combination code and listened for the beep. When the safe beeped and the lock clicked, I pulled back the small, heavy metal door. Yancy was still yapping from behind me, but all of a sudden I couldn't hear her. My ears were ringing. My heart pounded. I rubbed my eyes to make sure they weren't deceiving me. Heat rose from my feet and climbed up my body until it exploded out of the top of my head.

"Fuck!!!" I hollered. "Fucking bitch!!"

The safe was empty but for a lone piece of paper. I reached inside with a shaky hand and grabbed the paper. It was a note from Lauren. I held it between my fingers, but I couldn't even bring myself to read it.

"No! I told you! No!" Yancy cried out. She snatched the paper from my hand and began reading it out loud.

Dear Matt,

I guess by now you've figured out that I'm gone and that I've taken the money too. You had this coming to you. I think right now you feel the same way I felt when I found out about you fucking Yancy. Yes, that's right. I knew all along. I've been wanting to get back at you, and stiffing you for three million dollars is the ultimate fuck you.

I hope you realize that you lost a good one. Maybe you can put that whore Yancy back out on the track to make you some money. You'll never find another one like me, boo.

Sending a big FUCK YOU to you and her.
Lauren
P.S. Life with these millions is going to be
the shit! I hope you enjoy fucking that broke
bitch for the rest of your life.

Yancy stood stock still for a few seconds after she finished reading the letter. Then, as if someone had kicked her in the backs of her knees, she collapsed onto the closet floor.

"No, no, no!" Yancy shrieked over and over. She started kicking and screaming like that possessed bitch from the *Exorcist* movie. I couldn't even understand what she was saying, nor did I care.

"I'm going to kill that bitch! I will find her and I will kill her!" I screamed. I began going crazy, swiping clothes onto the floor, kicking over shoe boxes, and finally sending both of my fists through the long mirror on the back of the closet door. I was so angry, the pain from the glass cutting up my knuckles didn't even register. I punched the glass over and over until there was nearly no skin left on my knuckles.

"Lauren Kelly, you better hope I never find you. You fucked with the wrong man, you fucked with the wrong man," I said over and over. I didn't care if I died trying, I was going to find Lauren and blow her brains out.

"You let this happen!" Yancy screamed at

me. "You promised me that you would take care of it. You're so fucking stupid!"

Her words exploded in my ears like someone had detonated bombs in them. I grabbed a fistful of Yancy's weave and pulled her up from the floor.

"Get the fuck out!" I roared, dragging her toward the door. My hangover symptoms were long gone. I no longer had the pain in my head or the weak feeling in my body. I was feeling like the Incredible Hulk. My adrenaline was high, and I felt like I could snap someone in half with my bare hands.

"Get off of me! I'm not leaving until I get my money!" Yancy cried out. She swung her arms wildly, trying to break free. She twisted around, trying to bite, kick, and punch me.

"You better stop and just get the fuck out!" I roared. With the anger I was feeling, I knew that if I really hit her, the blow would be fatal. Once we reached the front door, I opened it and tossed her out by her hair. She fell forward onto her hands and knees.

"Matthew, you will see me again! This is not over!" Yancy cried. "This is not over! You motherfucka! It's not over!"

I wasn't trying to hear none of that bullshit she was spewing. I had too much shit on my mind to even care what Yancy was yapping about. I slammed the door in her face. Once I was inside my condo alone, I put my back against the door and slid down to the floor. I felt like a bitch sitting there with my knees pulled up into my chest, rocking back and forth. For the first time since my moms had had her head blown off right in front of me, I cried. I had not felt this kind of pain, grief, anger, and betrayal since that day, but now all of those emotions were back. I was crushed. Lauren had really hurt me. I wasn't the type that could take this kind of hurt and just bounce back like shit ain't happened. Nah, I still had pride. I still had an ego too.

"This ain't over. Somebody gotta die. Either you or me," I said through clenched teeth, speaking to Lauren as if she could actually hear me. "Somebody gotta die."

Don't Miss

Queen Divas
by De'nesha Diamond

*It's scorched-earth, all-or-nothing war for
Memphis' most merciless ride-or-die women, and
even their survival skills are no guarantee. And
once alliances splinter and explosive revelations rip
apart their empire, one diva's revenge will become
the ultimate deadly reign . . .*

Coming in April 2016

1

Mack

I've been in the game a long time as a Vice Lord Flower and I've seen my share of some fuckery, but I have to admit, even if it's just to myself, that nothing has prepared me for the shit that has gone down tonight. My girls Romil and Dime had joined forces to help the newest member of our crew, Ta'Shara Murphy, get her whacked-out sister, LeShelle, off of her back.

Why the fuck not? The bitch has spent the past year tryna murk Ta'Shara first, so it was the least that we could do. Actually, the order was: LeShelle ordered Ta'Shara gang raped for dating the brother of an enemy to her man. Ta'Shara attacked LeShelle with a pair of sewing needles at the mental hospital that her rape landed her in. LeShelle escaped police custody at a hospital to kill Ta'Shara's foster parents as revenge. And then the two were engaged in a contest to see who would who next.

Romil, Dime and I agreed to help. Of course it was only after we were drawn into killing two from our set: Qiana Barrett and GG.

I'm still not trying to think about that shit too much. Their murders happened so fast, it's still hard to wrap my brain around it. There was something about Qiana making a deal with LeShelle.

First of all, LeShelle Murphy was the head bitch in charge of the Queen Gs, the female gang that holds down the Gangster Disciples and also the sworn enemies of our gang the Vice Lord Flowers.

Qiana had no business making *any* deal with that crazy bitch so she got what she deserved. The deal was for LeShelle to kill Essence in return for Qiana killing her man's baby momma. But Qiana did more than kill a pregnant bitch, she sliced the girl's baby out and brought him over to Ruby Cove to raise—like a dumb ass.

So of course LeShelle Murphy cried foul and was threatening Qiana's life if she didn't return the baby.

The webs we weave when we practice to deceive.

After Qiana's confession, Ta'Shara attacked Qiana with a bottle of Johnnie Walker and then pushed the girl into a table loaded with candles, or maybe she tripped. I forget which. All I know is that the girl ran out of my living room looking like a human torch before she keeled over in my backyard. By the time I got the water hose working, the chick was dead.

GG, who'd brought Qiana's ass over to my crib for help with her LeShelle situation, then turned in a rage toward Ta'Shara, but she never made it back into the house before Dime put two slugs in the girl.

Dime claimed it was payback for Ta'Shara saving her life when a store owner went all jihad on them a few weeks back.

Regardless, this left my ass with two dead bodies in my house that we had to get rid of. Now, I'm not normally down for plugging our own, *but* Qiana did confess to killing a fellow Vice Lord Flower, Tyneisha, while doing a job for, of all people, LeShelle—so maybe there's a case to be made that the bitch deserved what she got. I don't know. Street politics can get tricky sometimes.

There was also one other piece of valuable information that Qiana gave before Ta'Shara lit her ass, and that was the exact place she was supposed to meet up with LeShelle. Knowing when and where to find that bitch was like hitting the lottery.

Still, when we rolled up into Hack's Crossing, the shit didn't go down like I thought it would. We had to play out a whole cat-and-mouse thing and take out two other Queen G bitches before we were able to snatch Le-Shelle. Ta'Shara's ass went straight psycho on our asses. She didn't kill her sister like a normal gangster bitch. She drew the shit out and tortured LeShelle while she was hogtied to a chair out in a warehouse building. Ta'Shara interrogated LeShelle and blasted holes into the girl each time the bitch said something that she didn't like. Ta'Shara ordered us to bring her boy Profit to the party because he needed to see the shit, too, since LeShelle had pumped a whole clip into his ass about a year back.

Profit wasn't the only thing that Ta'Shara wanted brought back to the warehouse. She wanted a can of gasoline. I thought she'd use it *after* she killed the girl. I never dreamed that she would light her ass up *while* the girl was still alive. The next few minutes were like something out of a horror movie. Ta'Shara doused LeShelle's helpless ass with the gasoline and tossed a match like she was unwanted trash.

LeShelle's screams are fucking with my ass. It was different from the way Qiana raced out of here. It's hard to describe it. The sound curdled my blood. I doubt that I'll ever forget that shit or the triumphant look on Ta'Shara's face.

There was no love lost between the sisters.

We dropped Ta'Shara alone off at Profit's crib. While he got rid of the human barbeque, Romil, Dime, and myself holed up at my place, marinating our livers and snorting lines of this bomb-ass coke.

After my third line, I *still* can't get that bitch's screams out of my head.

"You gonna get that?" Dime asks, lifting up her big head from the arm of my couch.

"Uh?"

"Your phone. Don't you hear it ringing?"

"My phone?" I look around, slow to see my phone on the table next to the last line of coke. "Shit." I fumble with the screen and answer the call before it goes to voicemail.

"Yeah?"

"Wake your ass up," Ta'Shara says. "Come and get me."

"Where you at?"

"Where do you think?"

Fuck. She's really going to leave Profit. "You sure?"

"I called you, didn't I?"

Aww. Shit. I look around for where I last placed my car keys.

"What the fuck?" Ta'Shara snaps.

"What?"

"Not you," she says, sounding distracted. "Hey, Mack. Let me call you back."

Click.

"You still want me to come and get you?"

Silence.

"Hello? Ta'Shara, are you still there?"

No answer.

When I still don't hear anything, I pull the phone from my ear and see that the call has been disconnected. "Well, shit."

"Who was that?" Romil asks, slurring her words.

"Ta'Shara." I toss the phone aside and lower my head back against my favorite La-Z-Boy.

"*Now* what does she want?"

"A ride. Looks like she and Profit are really gonna call it quits."

"Shit. She's a damn fool," Romil says, shaking her head. "Hell, if I was a few years younger, my ass would give her a fucking run for her money."

I laugh. "You and me both."

Dime stands when her fantasy boo, Trey Songz, plays on the radio. The fact that her ass is off beat doesn't faze her in the least. "So, are you going to run over there and get her or what?"

The fact that Ruby Cove is less than five minutes away is a plus right now. "I guess. You girls rolling with me?"

Romil moans like she's reluctant to un-ass her chair. "Do we have to? I mean. Damn. How many favors can a bitch ask for in one night?"

"You ain't gotta go—but somebody should

make sure that my ass don't fall asleep behind the wheel."

"I'll roll with you," Dime says, rolling her hips and snapping her fingers. I don't know whether she's trying to get tonight's wild episode out of her mind or if she's celebrating a couple of good kills tonight.

I'm more concerned about the changes I've witnessed in Ta'Shara. When we met her ass, she was a like a scared rabbit about to take on some Queen Gs on lockdown in the county jail. Now she's dropping bodies like she was born into the life. I don't know why that shit bothers me—but it does. Deep down, I want to see *somebody* make it out of the game— alive. Ta'Shara doesn't belong in 'the life,' but like it's been since the beginning of time, the streets change muthafuckas. There is no getting out.

"Well?" Dime stops dancing.

"Well, what?"

"Are we gonna ride through and pick T up?"

"Shit." My ass forgot just that damn quick. I push up out of my seat, dropping my phone and car keys on the floor.

Romil and Dime laugh. I flash them the bird before bending over to pick the items up. I'm far from being steady on my feet as I head to the door.

Dime asks, "Are you sure that your ass can even fucking drive?"

"I got this," I boast, struggle to put the key into the ignition.

"I'll drive," Dime declares, snatching the keys out of my hands and then shoving me.

"Fine. Fine. Fuck it. You drive." We have a big laugh as we exchange seats and then cruise toward Ruby Cove.

Grab the Hottest Fiction
from
Dafina Books

Grab These Novels by
Zuri Day

Available Wherever Books Are Sold!

All available as e-books, too!

Visit our website at **www.kensingtonbooks.com**